KINGS
OF
FATE

THE FURYCK SAGA: A PREQUEL NOVELLA

A.E. RAYNE

For more information about A.E. Rayne
and her upcoming books visit:
www.aerayne.com
/aerayne

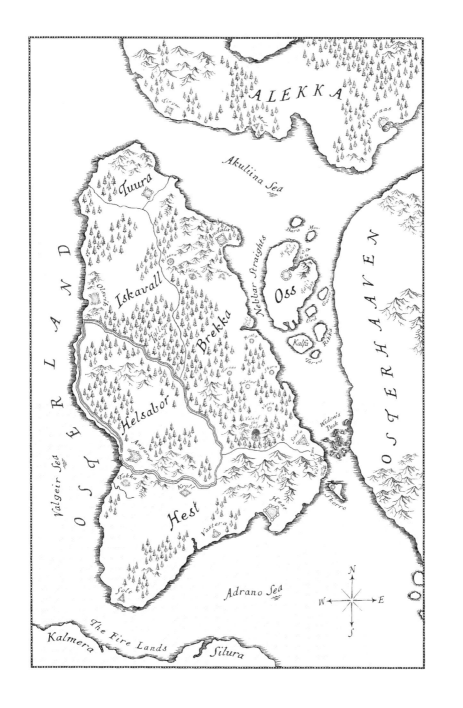

CHARACTERS

THE KINGDOM OF BREKKA

In Andala

Jael Furyck

Aleksander Lehr

King Lothar Furyck

Osbert Furyck

Gudrum Killi

Brynna 'Biddy' Halvor

Edela Saeveld

Gisila Furyck

Gant Olborn

Amma Furyck

Oleg Grenal

Jonas Elstan

Isaak Alfarr

Tiras

THE KINGDOM OF THE SLAVE ISLANDS

The Island of Oss

Eadmund Skalleson

King Eirik Skalleson

Eydis Skalleson

Thorgils Svanter

Morac Gallas

King Ake Bluefinn

Lord Hector Berras

Lady Cotilde Berras

Orla Berras

Evaine Gallas

Runa Gallas

Entorp Bray

Torstan Berg

Sevrin Jorri

PROLOGUE

The figure in the dark-brown cloak was tall.

A woman, Eydis thought, studying her closely as she approached.

Dark hair hung down to the middle of her back, the sides finely braided, tied with thin leather thongs.

Her cloak flapped away from her, and the woman turned, eyes on the muddy hill that ran down to the black stone beach. Those eyes were full of angry fire.

She didn't look happy.

Reaching inside her cloak, she wrapped her right hand around the hilt of a sword, and Eydis saw her straighten a pair of broad shoulders and jut out her chin. She had a serious face; attractive; strong. Her nose was straight and determined; her eyes intensely green. Eydis noticed a scar running under her right eye, and she blinked, suddenly intimidated. Looking down, she saw that the woman was wearing brown trousers tucked into mud-splattered boots, which she dug into the stones as if trying to disappear beneath them.

Flurries of snow blew across the beach, though in her dream, Eydis could not feel the chill of that bitter wind. But the woman could. She shivered, reluctantly releasing her hold on the sword, gathering her thin-looking cloak around her. She wasn't dressed for Oss, Eydis thought, watching the woman narrow her eyes until her frown left a deep indentation between her eyebrows, before sighing and starting the long walk across the slippery stones, towards the hill.

Eydis watched her go, holding her breath as the wind cried a painful song around her.

As the gods came to watch them both.

CHAPTER ONE

Jael Furyck could never decide who she hated more.

Her wet hair dripped onto her plate, soaking a lump of mashed turnips, though she didn't care; she detested turnips. Her green eyes were fixed on the men sitting at the high table: her uncle, Lothar the Usurper, a bloated, scheming old crook; his son, Osbert, a weasely leech. Gant Olborn was there too, neither scheming nor weasely, but the man who had helped them both take Brekka away from her younger brother, Axl, after their father's death. And though Axl did not appear to be turning into a man worthy of that throne any time soon, he was still the one her father had chosen to rule Brekka.

Two years since Ranuf Furyck's death and Jael still couldn't let it go.

She doubted she ever would, not while Lothar sat on the throne, destroying everything her father had worked so hard to build.

'You want to go?' Aleksander had nudged Jael, but she appeared in a dream, staring at the high table. He didn't blame her, but it wouldn't help any of them to live in the past.

It was long gone now.

Jael spun around, surprised to see him there. But Aleksander was usually beside her – in the hall, the training ring, in their bed – when he wasn't off hunting. They'd been inseparable since they were children. Since Aleksander's parents had been killed, and he'd been raised by her own. Jael frowned, dark eyebrows sharp. 'May as well. I'd rather be in that shit cottage than sitting here for Lothar's entertainment. Biddy's better company, and a much better cook.' She turned back to the high table, still surprised not to see her father up there, a moody scowl on his weathered face. He had been the most famous man in Osterland, a man strong enough in character and skill to have commanded Brekka for thirty years with no real challenge to his reign. His sudden death had left a void that someone as empty as Lothar could never fill.

Jael threw back the last of her ale and adjusted her sword belt. 'Let's go.'

Lothar's eyes followed her as she pushed her way through the flame-lit hall, heading for the doors, his moist lips wrinkling with displeasure. His temperamental niece continued to be a nagging problem. If only he could think of how to get rid of her without damaging his own standing. The people of Brekka would not tolerate her sudden demise, not at his hands at least. No, he had to remain far removed from whatever tragedy eventually befell the only daughter of his dead brother. Lothar reached for another oyster, slipping it into his quivering mouth, eyes still on his niece who had stopped by the giant smoke-stained doors, watching as they opened. And ushered in by a surprisingly cold gust of wind, came a tall, burly man swathed in a hooded cloak, dark-grey beard dripping, four men following behind him, the doors scudding closed after them all.

The man threw back his wet hood, yellow-tinged brown eyes gleaming as they fixed on the king in the distance. 'My lord!' he called, striding towards the fire which beckoned warmth and light before him. It was late summer, though it appeared that winter was already flexing its muscles, for the chill of the evening had seeped into his bones, and he couldn't stop his teeth chattering like an old woman.

Jael stumbled back in surprise, banging into Aleksander who grabbed her arms, feeling her body tense.

The man held his hands to the dancing flames of the fire, turning around, his gaze briefly on Jael. His smile grew as he ran a hand over his wet hair which was darker than his beard; recently cut short to get rid of a bad case of lice. He turned back around, eager for those crackling flames.

His equally bedraggled, shivering men fanned out around the fire pit behind him, wet hands extended, hungry eyes skipping from the flames to the trays of salted herring and oysters being delivered to the high table.

'Gudrum!' Lothar struggled to his feet, surprised but pleased to see his old friend.

'Lothar!' Gudrum poured himself a cup of ale and headed for the high table, draining it quickly, ignoring the scowl he could feel following him.

He didn't turn around.

He had seen that face in his mind for years.

That bitch's face.

Let her stew, he thought. Let her wonder.

And slamming his cup down on the table, he opened his arms and strode towards the King of Brekka.

Jael watched Lothar embrace him. The noise in the hall, momentarily quietened by the surprise arrival, was suddenly loud again, and she could feel Aleksander tugging her arm, attempting to drag her out the door.

Gudrum clapped Gant on the back as he squeezed onto the bench beside him, next to Lothar who returned to his high-backed, fur-lined chair. 'It's been a long time, old friend,' he grinned, showing off a full set of teeth, cramped tightly together, even yellower than his eyes. His round face was still dripping with rain, and grabbing a used napkin from the table, Gudrum wiped it over his hairy round cheeks, rubbing his beard. He threw the cloth back on the table and smiled, taking in the familiar sight of Andala's King's Hall.

Ten years since he'd last been here. Ten years of imagining this moment.

Gant's smile was slow to arrive, but he could see Lothar watching him, so he bit down on his distaste and made an effort. Though he had grown up with Gudrum, the man was no friend of his; never had been. He was useful with a sword – more than useful, he admitted grudgingly – but Gant had always doubted the strength of his character. Though, staring at the hall doors as Jael and Aleksander disappeared outside, he knew that he was the last one to talk, sitting alongside Lothar the Usurper as he was.

'Where are you headed?' Lothar wondered, flicking a chubby finger at his harried steward who struggled over, slopping two jugs of ale onto the table. 'Or is this my long overdue visit you've been promising for years?'

'Ha!' Gudrum's thick shoulders relaxed, his body sinking towards the table. He was a sizeable man, still in his prime, lethal with a sword, with a knife, with any weapon he could lay his hands on. He killed, could kill, would kill for the right price. And he had. And over the years he'd become a wealthy man, though he'd grown bored with serving kings. First, Ranuf Furyck, then Hugo Vandaal in Iskavall, and though Lothar had wanted him by his side in Andala, Brekka's capital, he was ready to forge a new path now. To find his own seat of power across the sea.

But there was just one thing he needed to attend to first.

'I wanted to see you, of course,' Gudrum grinned, the lines of his grizzled face deep like the folds in a cloth. A thick scar ran down from his receding hairline, through his left eyebrow just past the corner of his eye. 'Ramon Vandaal has no use for my services any longer, which is no surprise, of course. Ravenna never liked me. She was always in his ear, despite the best efforts of your sweet daughter, so he let me go.'

Lothar sat up in surprise, readjusting his straining belt. He saw his youngest daughter, Amma, emerge from behind the grey curtain that separated the hall from the bedchambers, though he didn't acknowledge her as he turned back to Gudrum. 'Oh?'

'I hold no grudge against the boy. He's weak and spineless, and knowing Ollsvik as we both do, he'll soon be dead,' Gudrum growled with some satisfaction, eyes on the tray of oysters Lothar was picking at, his cold lips moist with hunger. 'I shall set my own course now. See where the wind takes me. As long as it's far away from Osterland, I'll be happy. I've enough bad memories here to never need to see the place again. '

Lothar's worry about his son-in-law was quickly surpassed by his curiosity. 'You're taking a ship?'

Gudrum nodded.

Osbert coughed, gagging, a fishbone stuck in his throat. He was just as curious about Gudrum's plans as his father, though neither man had even acknowledged him yet.

Lothar frowned, irritated by Osbert's coughing, though his attention remained on Gudrum. 'A ship to where?'

'Up north. Alekka to start with, maybe further, up into The Murk.'

'That far?' Gant bent forward, finally intrigued himself. 'It's a bit wild up there, isn't it?' He filled his cup, offering the ale jug to Gudrum who took it with a nod, filling his own.

Gudrum scanned the hall, checking on his men who'd helped themselves to stools around the fire, and were now being attended to by Lothar's servants. He sat back with a shrug. 'Free, you mean. Plenty of opportunities for a man to make a name for himself. Land, land, and more land! All for the taking. If you've got enough coins and skilled men with weapons, you can make a fortune. Make your own rules.'

'If you can stomach the cold! You'll have balls the size of peas!' Lothar snorted, slapping Osbert on the back, desperate to shut him up. 'Balls the size of peas, and cannibals looking to serve them up for supper!'

'Ha!' Gudrum's laugh was a low rumble in his belly. 'You believe those tales, old friend?' He ran a hand through his beard, wringing water onto the floor. 'Tales to scare children, not men. Not men with swords and axes. Men who've been knee-deep in blood since they were weaned from their mother's tit.'

Lothar saw the hungry look in Gudrum's eyes, and he felt a twinge, not wanting a warrior that hard and sharp to slip through his fingers again. He had tried without luck to lure him back to Andala when he'd made his move on the throne. He'd wanted Gudrum beside him then, helping him push back against Jael and any resistance she would mount against his rule. Though, in truth, she had offered little. Nothing of any substance. Not yet, at least. 'So, how long will you be staying, then? Long enough for me to change your mind, perhaps?'

Gudrum laughed. 'You think you can change my mind, Lothar Furyck? I wish you the luck of the gods trying! I'll stay a couple of days. Enough time to sort a few things out.' His eyes were up, watching the doors swing open. A small man he recognised skulked in, dripping hood hanging low, face hidden in flame-tipped shadows. Tiras. How that snivelling worm was still alive was anyone's guess. Though a snivelling worm was the perfect spy for a slug king. He smiled at Lothar. 'But enough about me, old friend. How are things with you?'

Gant heard Lothar belch in response before dipping his head towards Gudrum, lowering his voice. If he'd wanted to, Gant could have tried to hear what he was saying. No doubt something about Jael. About Aleksander and Axl.

He sighed, grey eyes skipping past Lothar and Gudrum to Osbert who had recovered from his choking fit, and was now busy molesting one of the servants whose eyes were dull with resignation as his hand slipped inside the bodice of her worn dress. Gant clenched his jaw, knowing there was little he could do about that. Lothar both despised and enabled his only son. He would never take anyone's side against him; not his precious heir, the one who would rule after his death, whenever that might be.

Gant tried to clear his mind, but a storm of memories swirled around him with ever-increasing ferocity. He saw Tiras, who had crept around the bed-lined walls of the hall, edging his way behind the dais and Lothar's chair, where he waited in the shadows.

Gant felt his shoulders creeping up to his ears, wrenched with discomfort.

Wondering what Jael was going to do about Gudrum.

***

'You can't do anything about Gudrum!' Aleksander insisted, dark eyes glowing like coal in the flames.

Their servant, Biddy, fussed around the fire, trying not to burn her fingers as she readjusted the logs, hoping to encourage more light in their miserable cottage. Sparks flew. 'There's barely enough room to sneeze in this box,' she grumbled, rubbing a sooty hand across a furrowed brow. Biddy had her bed fur wrapped around her shoulders, so there was only a threadbare sheet covering the straw-stuffed mattress on her tiny bed. She sat down with a thump, listening to the straw crackle beneath her.

With Jael and Aleksander eating in the hall, she had not bothered to make much supper for herself; just a few slices of cheese and some stale crispbreads. Her stomach rumbled in protest, though, so she bent to look under her bed, hoping she still had a few plums ferreted away.

Jael ignored her, wobbling on her stool, trying to ignore Aleksander too. 'Gudrum came back for me,' she muttered. 'I've no choice but to do something about him.'

'You don't know that for sure,' Aleksander said, watching the scar under Jael's eye twitch as she grew more incensed. 'He's thick with Lothar. Has been since he left Andala. He was his man in Ollsvik. Perhaps he's just come for a visit?'

'Ha! Thick with Lothar? And he's only coming to see him now?' Jael ran a hand through one of her braids, trying to unravel it. The wind had tangled her hair into a bramble bush, and she needed to get a comb through it before it became impossible. 'No, he's here because of me. You know that.'

'Why?' Biddy sat up, nibbling an over-ripe plum, suddenly interested in their conversation. 'Why does Gudrum want you?' She was slightly older than Jael's mother, Gisila, though she felt like an old woman already. Her aches and pains seemed to multiply with each passing day, and her mind was struggling to keep afloat as their lives continued to sink. Day by day, bit by bit, Lothar and his vile son were working to make everything untenable, wanting to provoke a reaction. Biddy didn't know how much more Jael could take. Or Axl. Especially Axl. It was his throne Lothar was squatting on. His kingdom that Lothar was using to enrich himself.

How much longer would it be before Jael or Axl did something to get themselves killed?

'You don't remember?' Aleksander wondered, turning around to Biddy whose brown curls bounced around a worn face.

Biddy frowned, eyes widening as memories flickered. 'His boy? What was his name? Ronal? He's the one who killed Asta!'

Jael nodded, running a whetstone down her long blade. The sword had been her father's – the Furyck sword – passed down through generations of kings, and now to her. Ranuf may have inexplicably left Axl his throne, but he had, at least, left her his sword. 'And now Gudrum's come for me. And what am I going to do about that?' She looked up, staring into Aleksander's eyes, searching for some clue as to what he thought.

They were so close that they usually knew what the other was thinking.

'Nothing,' Aleksander insisted, dark hair falling over an angular face, jaw working hard as he leaned towards the flames, warming his hands. 'We're only safe here for now. Lothar chooses to let you live, you and Axl, until he doesn't. You do something now, you risk both your lives. Gisila and Edela. Biddy. All of us.'

Jael's chin was throbbing where he'd punched her earlier during training. Her boots were wet through and, in the rundown cottage where the wind was whistling through gaps in the crumbling wattle-and-daub walls, and the rain was dripping down the smoke hole splashing the flames, she felt cold, though her body vibrated with anger.

Gudrum Killi thought he would come for her.

Now?

After all these years?

She swept the whetstone down her blade again, watching its sharp edge glint in the spitting flames.

Last time they'd seen each other, Gudrum had been one of her father's finest warriors. And she had been a girl.

The girl who had killed his bastard son.

And now there was going to be a reckoning.

***

Osbert had no love for his cousin.

That wasn't true.

Osbert had nothing but love for his cousin. He saw her in his dreams. And in his dreams she was naked, writhing on top of him, lying beneath him, bent over before him.

But she was so arrogant. Reckless. Brash.

The first female born in the Furyck's long and noble line.

She thought that made her better than anyone.

Furia's daughter, they called her. Furia, the Goddess of War.

Osbert's hand slipped off the door handle. Lothar had been so pleased to see Gudrum that he'd ordered his best wine brought to the high table, which had surprised Osbert, who'd greedily helped himself to cup after cup until his bleary-eyed father had somehow gathered his senses and sent his steward to return the barrel to his locked storage room.

Turning at the sound of a panicked squeak, Osbert saw Lothar, head buried in the bosom of the pretty servant he'd planned to take to his own bed. Myra. Such soft lips. Like warm cream. He felt a stab of jealousy. Anger too. His mother was barely dead. His father had not even made a show of mourning her. Though, in truth, he'd behaved no differently while the poor woman was alive.

Osbert gripped the door handle firmly now as his father dragged Myra towards his chamber, his generous girth jiggling in anticipation of the pleasures that awaited within.

'You!' Lothar bellowed, shuddering to a stop, his head swinging around. 'My son! You will meet me in the square in the morning. Gudrum and I have planned something you'll want to see, I'm sure. Best you get some rest now. I don't want you to miss it!'

Osbert frowned, too angry and jealous, and far too drunk to feel curious. His father was his king, and one day, he knew, the Brekkan throne would be his. At twenty-four years old, Osbert was hungry for power, ready to escape from under his father's oppressive thumb.

Ambitious and impatient too.

He was small and wiry, no great warrior admittedly, though his mind was sharper than most and he was a Furyck, born to rule. And he would, when his father died.

If not before.

Osbert puckered his lips, feeling the sway of his body as thoughts turned away from his father, and the loss of the desirable Myra, to the comfortable bed that awaited him in his chamber.

And his mind wandered straight back to Jael.

***

Their bed was narrow. Narrower than anything a servant would sleep in, at least when Ranuf had been the King of Brekka.

Their noses almost touched as they worked to keep their voices low, not wanting Biddy to hear. They weren't trying to keep secrets, not from Biddy who had raised Jael since she was a baby, and Aleksander since he was ten. Secrets were impossible in the close confines of the tiny cottage, but neither of them wanted to worry her.

There was already enough to worry about.

'Gudrum said there would be a reckoning. When I killed Ronal, he said there would be a reckoning,' Jael whispered, feeling around her aching chin, her cold legs wrapped around Aleksander's warm ones. 'And here it is.'

Despite the pleasurable feeling of those familiar cold legs rubbing against his, Aleksander felt tense. 'We don't know for certain that that's why he's come.'

'We do. *I* do. We need to be prepared.'

'Prepared for what?'

'For what Lothar will do when I kill Gudrum.'

'Jael.' Aleksander squeezed her free hand.

'Go to sleep,' she whispered, kissing him quickly, untangling her legs. 'Go to sleep.' And then, seemingly changing her mind, her lips lingered on his. 'I know what he wants,' she murmured, moving closer, pressing her body against Aleksander's. 'He wants revenge.'

Aleksander ran a hand over her sharp cheekbone, smoothing her newly braided hair away from her face. The glow from the banked fire was dull, but he knew that face better than anyone's. It was a beautiful face, scowls and scars and all. Mesmerising green eyes, moody lips that hadn't curled into a smile much since Ranuf's death. That scar.

An unforgiving face. A face he adored.

'He may want you, but he can't have you,' he breathed, kissing her.

'No,' Jael agreed, her eyes wide open, 'he can't. I won't let him.'

CHAPTER TWO

'She certainly catches the eye,' Eirik Skalleson mused, winking at his old friend.

'She does. Though Eadmund would need to be awake to notice,' Morac Gallas suggested, suffering a moody scowl in return for his honest assessment.

The two old men stood, ankle-deep in mud, watching Hector Berras, Lord of Blixo, escort his wife and daughter around Oss' blustery square. It was a truly miserable day, and Eirik could taste snow in the air, though winter itself was months away. But despite the dour morning, Oss' king felt a burst of enthusiasm.

For the first time in years, he felt like a true king.

Mostly, he felt like a parent, settling disputes, punishing and reprimanding. Praising. Trying to inspire. Imposing rules, hoping to achieve some order.

He felt like a crotchety father, wanting to be alone.

But today he was not just entertaining the famed King of Alekka, Ake Bluefinn, he was also hosting some of that king's most important lords; those men Ake trusted beside him in battle. Scarred, hard men he had lifted out of the blood and guts of victory, taking them with him to Stornas, Alekka's capital, where he had claimed the Alekkan throne from the tyrannical king he'd been waging war against since his youth.

And since his ascension to the throne, fifteen years ago, Ake had ruled with a generous hand. Benevolent and kind to his people, scornful and intolerant of his enemies, until now, when he had proposed a truce, and a meeting to discuss the prospect of an alliance with his old foe across the Akuliina Sea.

Oss was the largest of the eight islands in Eirik Skalleson's kingdom; his home since his birth as a slave, sixty-two years ago. The home he had transformed from a colony of depraved slavers and their abused prisoners into a kingdom of free men and women, with the help of his best friend and closest advisor, Morac Gallas.

Now they stood in Eirik's stone fort, wrinkled old men.

Eirik's blonde hair was almost all white; Morac's as grey as the sky above them. Their children were grown, and now the future of the islands was coming into sharper relief. And they both worried about who would sit on the throne after Eirik was gone.

Eirik thought about it daily. Hourly, if he were honest.

He felt sick at the thought of leaving his kingdom in the hands of his son Eadmund, who was in no state to command a horse, let alone an entire kingdom. Eirik needed to find him a wife. Someone to guide him. To care for him.

To knock him into shape.

He'd tried for years to turn Eadmund around.

They'd all tried – his friends, his sister – but nothing had helped.

His son remained a useless mess, trapped in a world of ale and despair.

Eirik sighed, wrinkling his forehead, trying to hold down his flapping white beard. He'd weighted it down with silver nuggets, endeavouring to fight back against Oss' howling gales, but he obviously needed to use more. 'I'm happy with Eadmund sleeping. He can sleep all day long while the Alekkans are here. Let him hibernate. He can come out in spring!'

Morac's smile barely moved his thin lips. He was a morose man, getting more so as his scars and battle wounds turned into aches and pains in the bitter cold that was Oss. Each year, spring and summer would whip by in a frigid sea wind, before ushering in a bleak and bitter winter that would freeze them in for months. He too could taste snow in the air, and his shoulders slumped at the thought of it. 'Eadmund probably thinks you're going to try and make a match for him again,' Morac said casually, his eyes back on the girl. Not a girl, he thought. She carried herself like a woman. A lady. There was nothing shy or childlike about her. Her orange hair glowed like flames as she walked, her smile bright against the dull sky.

It was hard to look away.

'Well, he'd be wrong about that,' Eirik laughed, though his eyes held his friend's gaze with some regret. 'Ake's daughters are children, promised to the sons of his lords.' Eirik dropped his voice as the Berras family turned to walk their way. 'Though it does seem odd to bring the girl here unless you have some intention...'

Morac's frown was severe. He didn't want to encourage his king down that treacherous path. It was better for the islands if their alliance with Alekka didn't hinge on Eadmund and a woman. 'I don't imagine it would serve you well to make that match, old friend,' he murmured. 'Not if you want to keep Ake on side. Eadmund has a way of... causing problems.' He flinched, expecting Eirik to snap, but their guests arrived before he could say a word.

'I feel as though we've entered another season entirely!' Lord Hector Berras boomed as he stopped before the two men, clapping red hands against his cloaked arms, breath smoke floating around a broad, cheerful face. 'When we left Stornas, the sun was out. We were almost contemplating removing our cloaks, weren't we, Orla?' He was a substantial man; completely bald, with a red birthmark covering almost half his head. He smiled generously, though his hooded blue eyes were always watchful, especially when his daughter was nearby, leaving Eirik in no doubt that his guest was constantly weighing everything he heard and saw with a blade-sharp mind.

Orla, his orange-haired daughter, laughed, and Eirik took note of her full set of teeth. Freckles too. '*You* were, Father,' she said, round cheeks revealing deep dimples. 'I can't imagine ever taking *my* cloak off in Stornas!' She glanced at her mother who looked awkward as she tittered beside her, too shy to make eye contact with anyone, hiding beneath a fussy hairstyle of intricately beaded braids that had slumped forward and was now hanging over her eyes.

Hector Berras stared at his wife with a frown, trying to draw her attention to the malfunctioning hairstyle. He was a wealthy man. Wealthier than the King of Alekka and the King of Oss put together, he was sure, and though that wealth could buy dresses and jewels, it could not buy his timid wife any confidence or style. He smiled awkwardly, wishing he'd left her behind.

Morac coughed, and Eirik stopped staring at the girl, his attention drifting to his daughter, Eydis, who was walking slowly towards them, one hand out in front of her, trying to find her way.

Eirik lifted a boot out of the sucking mud and excused himself, heading towards his daughter, who was thirteen, blind, and thoroughly impossible to keep in one place. 'You're supposed to be using your stick!' he grumbled, grabbing Eydis' arm as she slipped. 'Did you imagine you would just lie in the mud, hoping someone would come by and pick you up?'

Eydis couldn't decide whether to frown or smile. She was a teenager, though, and feeling hungry, so a frown it was. 'I know the fort well enough, Father,' she grumbled. 'And only my sight is impaired. My legs work just fine.'

'I don't doubt it,' Eirik said, slipping her arm through his. 'But even those of us with two eyes are struggling today. The square's a bog. May as well just let in the cows!'

Eydis grinned, hearing the cheerfulness in her father's voice. He had not sounded that happy in some time, and then she realised why. 'It's that girl, isn't it?'

'What do you mean?' Eirik stopped, staring into his raven-haired daughter's eyes. They were milky white, had been from birth, but if she had not been born blind, Eirik was certain they would have shone a bright cornflower blue like her mother's had. He smiled sadly, thinking about Rada, his third wife. She had died giving birth when Eydis was only five-years-old. He had lost both a wife and son that day. The pain was still so raw that sometimes it felt as though it was only yesterday. 'What girl?' he wondered, blinking himself back into the present.

'The orange-haired girl. I saw her in my dreams.' Eydis wrinkled her nose, inhaling a fresh dump of manure, but as she turned her head away, the mouth-watering aroma of meat cooking on Ketil's grills wafted towards her, and she smiled. Ketil and his sister, Una, had the most popular spot in the square, serving up piping hot sticks of meat for freezing cold Osslanders each day.

'You did?' Eirik was intrigued. Eydis, like her mother, was a dreamer. Though blind while awake, she had always been able to see in her dreams: the future, the past, visions of what would come. Both helpful and terrifying, Eirik thought, his shoulders tense. 'What did you see?'

'Trouble.'

'Oh.' Eirik sought out Morac who was keeping the Berras family busy. He scanned the square, peering through the misty clouds grazing the tops of the ramparts crowning his stone fort. He couldn't see Ake Bluefinn, though he had likely gone back to the hall for more food. The Alekkan king appeared to be a man whose appetite was no longer for battle or glory, but for wine and whitefish and all those delicacies that Eirik's kingdom was known for, though Eirik could hardly fault him for that. In fact, he was encouraged to think that Ake appeared to have little interest in maintaining a war posture.

There was hope for the future of the islands in that.

But as for his dreamer daughter? 'What sort of trouble, Eydis?' he whispered, frowning as the rain started.

'I don't know,' she admitted, lifting the hood of her cloak to cover her dark hair. 'But you should stay well away from her, Father. Don't let yourself be talked into anything. It won't go well, you know Eadmund.'

Eirik pulled Eydis away from a man lugging a wide load of wattle on his back. Small stretches of woodland ran down the middle of the island, with quarries further south, so the tiny cottages crammed inside the fort were a mix of wattle-and-daub, with some older stone houses. Oss was a mostly barren island, and much of what they needed, that didn't come from the sea and the beaches, was imported from the other islands and Tuura; some parts of Alekka too.

Eirik frowned, trying to focus his thoughts which were suddenly as tangled as a pile of fishing line. As much as he wanted and needed to find his son a wife, it would do no good to cause problems with the Alekkans.

***

Brekka was a richly fertile kingdom, with undulating mountain ranges, and verdant plains, perfect for farming. The winters were bitter but not as bleak as they were up north in Tuura. The summers were mild, not suffocating as they were down in Hest. It was the kingdom all others wanted a piece of, and Ranuf Furyck had spent much of his long reign working to hold back invaders, trying to protect his people, to keep them safe, and ensure their prosperity.

Lothar, though, was a different type of leader. His beady eyes were fixed further afield. He was hungry to extend his borders, eager to claim victory over his southern neighbours, salivating at the prospect of ruling over the Kingdom of Hest one day. For though Brekka had land to farm, Hest had a harbour that wealthy merchants flocked to. Merchants, not traders. Merchants who brought silks, glass, and spices from the Fire Lands. Who had more gold and riches than all of the lords in Osterland combined.

And one day Lothar knew that he would claim it for Brekka.

If his niece didn't disrupt his plans.

He nudged a yawning Osbert into an upright position as Gudrum approached, leading a snorting black horse. They had been waiting in the middle of the square, which after the terrible weather of the past few days was starting to turn into a mucky field. 'Eh? What do you think about that, then?' Lothar chuckled, nudging his son some more.

Osbert swallowed, his mouth opening and closing as his father left him and waddled towards Gudrum, his fur-trimmed cloak sweeping the muddy ground. Turning around, Osbert surveyed the square, noting how many of the gathered Andalans appeared to be just as horrified by what Lothar had done.

And then he saw Jael approaching.

They had argued all the way from the cottage, Aleksander insisting that she shouldn't try to fight Gudrum; Jael already having decided that she would most definitely try to fight him. That was why he had come. He wanted revenge. He wanted her dead. And she would happily give him the opportunity to try and kill her. Why not?

It was the perfect way to end him.

Seeing Lothar grinning at her, and Osbert eyeing her slyly, Jael shivered to a stop, feeling Aleksander grip her arm.

Tig.

Gudrum turned around, his hooded eyes squinting, despite the lack of sunshine. He'd barely slept, and his entire face was puffy and bloated, but his smile was wide, and his pleasure in Jael's horror was energising.

Jael flung away Aleksander's hand and strode towards Gudrum, arms shaking, chest aching, white breath smoke pumping around her face. 'Uncle.' Her voice was quiet, clipped as she ignored both Gudrum and her beloved horse, Tig, her eyes snapping to Lothar who looked just as bleary-eyed but suddenly a lot less cocky than Gudrum. 'What is going on?' Heart pounding now, Jael curled her right hand into a fist to stop herself grabbing her sword. She could feel the long scabbard resting against her thigh, almost calling to her, urging her to act.

Then her father's voice in her ear. 'Jael...' She knew that tone. The one he'd always used when her temper started to flare. 'Jael... no.'

Lothar didn't speak. He didn't even pry his wet lips apart as he stood there beside Gudrum and the enormous black horse who was suddenly swinging his head around, trying to escape Gudrum's hold.

'Going on?' Gudrum stepped forward, sensing that Lothar's tongue had tangled in his mealy mouth as his niece towered threateningly over him. She had grown into a tall woman, he could see. Broad shoulders. Strong arms more than capable of wielding a sword against a bigger man. Her reputation had grown too. They had talked about Furia's daughter in every kingdom up and down Osterland for years; even more so since her father's death, wondering why Ranuf hadn't chosen to put her on the throne. 'Your uncle has kindly helped me solve a knot of a problem I've been working on for years.'

Jael waited, listening to the frantic gallop of her heart, feeling her body pulse in time, sensing Aleksander stop behind her. More and more Andalans were congregating in the gloomy square, quiet and curious, eyes fixed on Jael. Everyone knew what Tig meant to her. Ranuf had given that bad-tempered stallion to his daughter when she was a girl. Her first proper horse. They had been inseparable ever since.

Some whispered that Jael loved that horse more than anyone.

They would have been right.

Jael glared at Lothar who appeared to be shrinking into his cloak; the thick rolls of fat around his neck almost swallowing his globulous face. 'And what problem is that?' She turned to eye Gudrum, her voice iron-edged.

Lothar coughed, aware of what a public spectacle this was suddenly becoming. In the smoky darkness of the hall, with a cup of his best wine in an unsteady hand and the plump, delicious Myra squirming in his lap, Gudrum's proposal had sounded too perfect to resist.

Lothar had imagined the pleasure he would take in such a moment; the warm glow of delight he would feel watching his niece squirm. But now, in the bleak light of morning, with bile swilling around his mouth, and the silent judgment of the gathered Andalans all too obvious to see, he realised that he was walking the finest of lines. Clearing his throat, Lothar turned to the crowd, sweeping his arms around. 'Gudrum lost a son! You all know that! He is entitled to a blood price! Ranuf owed him that, but he refused! Gudrum, in his wisdom, left Andala, knowing that to stay would only cause problems. And now he has returned. Not for revenge!

But to claim that which is owed to him! What *you* owe him!' Lothar insisted, rounding on his niece. 'What *you* must pay!'

'And you think a horse can replace a son?' Jael tried to sound amused, her voice carrying across the square. 'He would rather have a horse than gold? Than revenge? Than my life?' She spun around, aware of the crowd, wanting their support. There were titters of amusement, smiles and nods. 'Tig is a skilled horse, I know, but even he couldn't hold a sword in battle!'

Laughter now; red-nosed, white-breathed Andalans laughing along with their former princess. The one who should have been their queen.

Lothar could feel their warmth towards Jael, and his face flushed with irritation. 'Gudrum is welcome to choose another price!' he decided, rethinking how much value there was in substituting a horse for the death of his niece. He would much rather get rid of the latter, and he'd never even noticed the former. 'Perhaps this *should* be settled with swords? It would seem only fair. And we all know how eager my niece is to use her sword!'

Sensing that everything was about to unravel, Osbert hurried forward, wanting to dissuade his father from making a catastrophic mistake. Giving away Jael's horse was a stupid idea that would endear him to no one. Offering her up to be killed was an even more foolhardy decision that he didn't want his father to make.

But Gudrum was quicker.

He was a man of occasion. He knew the power of a crowd; how easily the roar of displeasure could undo a weak leader's resolve. And Lothar had always been a weak, greedy man, which is why Ranuf had banished him from Brekka years ago. 'I have no desire to shed more blood! And I will not displease the gods by killing a Furyck! But my son is dead! All these years I have been without him, yet I have not sought revenge! And I seek none now! I only want a fair price for the loss of my boy!' His voice sounded full of pain, but Jael was close enough to see Gudrum's conniving eyes. She saw the hint of a smile teasing the corners of his bearded lips. And she could feel the pleasure he was taking from watching her squirm.

Tig threw back his head, wanting to go to Jael, and Gudrum yanked harshly on his reins.

Jael instinctively reached for her sword. She could hear the murmurs, sense the nods of acceptance that Gudrum was making not only a fair point but an honourable one. 'That may be so, but since my horse didn't kill your son, it doesn't seem like a fair price to me. Why punish him for something I did? Or is it that all your years in Iskavall have turned you soft, Gudrum Killi? There have been no songs sung about you, no stories told in the King's Hall that I remember. Warunda was here only last month, yet your name didn't pass his lips once. Is that because the boy on Iskavall's throne has no need for an old man who's lost his edge? If you ever had one in the first place!' Jael stepped forward, snarling. She could sense Gudrum trying to wheedle out of the trap she needed to force him into, and the one Lothar seemed happy to help her set.

She had to fight Gudrum. She had to kill him.

He couldn't take Tig.

Gudrum's eyes sparked with anger, and as he jerked forward, Lothar stepped back. He had spent a lot of time watching Gudrum fight over the years, and he knew that Jael was quite wrong in her assumptions. Gudrum Killi's skill with a sword had not diminished at all.

Gudrum twisted Tig's reins around a filthy hand, losing patience with the foul-tempered, skittery horse and his spitting owner. 'Perhaps I am not the man I was,' he growled, jaw clenched. 'After you killed Ronal, I was lost. My wife died of a broken heart, her only child murdered. So yes, without my family, what did I have left?' He shook his head, eyes up on the crowd again, seeking their favour. 'I have no desire to kill you, Jael. I don't wish to spill any blood to avenge my son. That won't bring him back. I'm leaving Osterland. Heading for Alekka and a new life. I want nothing else from you or your family.' He looked at Lothar, eyes suddenly misty. 'I only ask for this horse. To settle matters.'

Murmurs of sympathy grew.

'No!' Jael knew that she had lost the crowd, but there was nothing she could do about that now. She felt no sympathy for

Gudrum. His son had been a shit. A terrorising shit who had made her life miserable for years. Unhappy with continually being bested by her in the training ring, he had stalked her, waiting until she was alone. Wanting to humiliate her, to hurt her. Finding new ways to do just that, until he finally killed her beloved dog, right in front of her, his friends holding her back, making her watch. 'No!'

'It's a fair payment, Jael.' Osbert pushed himself in between Jael and Gudrum, much to his father's annoyance. Much to Tig's annoyance too, who shook his head, flinging a dark gob of snot at Osbert's eye.

The crowd laughed, and Lothar closed his eyes in embarrassment.

Jael didn't notice as she slipped a hand beneath her cloak, drawing out her sword. 'You will not take my horse!'

'Jael!'

Jael held her ground, eyes fixed on Gudrum, but Aleksander swung around to see the tiny figure of Edela Saeveld scurrying into the melee; a small old woman wrapped in a dark-red cloak, white hair blowing around a determined face. Squeezing her way in between Lothar, Gudrum, Osbert and Jael, and trying not to be stomped on by an increasingly irate Tig, Edela looked up at her granddaughter, placing a cold hand on her arm. 'It will do no good to start a fight over a horse,' she grumbled, trying to get Jael to focus on her. 'A horse? When poor Gudrum here lost his only son?'

Aleksander's mouth quickly fell open, mimicking Jael's; Lothar's and Osbert's too.

Jael's sword tip dipped slightly, her anger dampened by confusion. '*What*?'

'A price must be paid!' Edela insisted loudly, blue eyes sharp as she studied the equally confused crowd. 'And I'm afraid, Jael, despite how much you love your horse, you must pay it.'

Jael wondered if she was having a nightmare. Surely, she was dreaming?

Her shoulders slumped as she stepped back, away from her grandmother, away from Aleksander, sheathing her sword.

She was suddenly so cold.

All eyes were on her as she took one last look at Tig and spun around, pushing her way through the crowd, heading for the harbour gates.

Needing to be alone.

CHAPTER THREE

Eadmund Skalleson winced as he struggled into a sitting position, trying to focus on the enormous man who loomed over him like a red-headed standing stone. 'What?'

'You missed training,' Thorgils grumbled, scuffing the old floorboards with his muddy boots. His cloak dripped, and so did his nose. He wiped it on the back of a hand, sniffing as he glared down at his best friend with a pair of usually cheerful blue eyes. 'Again.'

Eadmund could hear rain on the roof, the wind screaming around the walls of... wherever he was. He couldn't remember. It was...

Shaking his head, he tried to clear his muddled thoughts, but he only ended up making his head throb more painfully. 'Training?' His throat was so dry that he could barely form words. He looked around for something to drink, but the ale jug lay on the floor beside his bed, empty, just like his head was.

Eadmund remembered now. His cottage. He was in his cottage.

The perfect place to escape his father's fussing. And usually that of his friends too. When he disappeared into the cottage, they knew to leave him alone.

Though, not today, it seemed.

'Sounds like a storm out there.' Thunder boomed overhead, and Eadmund bit his tongue in surprise.

'And?' Thorgils wasn't moving. 'How are you ever going

to make a change if you don't even try? Torstan's out in the Pit, waiting. And what have you been doing? Lying there, dreaming of ale? There's not even a woman in your bed! What are you lying there for, you useless arse?'

Eadmund coughed, easing his legs over the side of the creaking bed. He was almost thirty-years-old, but his body felt like that of an old man. Every limb hung heavily about him. He barely had the strength to lift an eyelid. 'What are you yelling at me for? There's a storm! Go to the hall! Find a bench. I'll be there soon.'

'Not so fast, my troublesome friend,' Thorgils said, searching for Eadmund's cloak. 'The hall's off-limits for drinking this morning. Eirik doesn't want his guests molested by the likes of you or me this early in the day.'

'Guests?' Eadmund frowned. It hurt. He felt a familiar ache in his stomach, and he sighed, equally full of regret and the desire for more ale. He took the cloak Thorgils had retrieved from the floor, noticing how filthy it was, how in need of repair. And with winter threatening to arrive early, he was going to have to do something about it soon. 'What guests?'

Memories flitted back of a time when he had been more than an embarrassment to his father; someone Eirik needed to hide away, out of sight.

'What do you mean, what guests?' Thorgils was incredulous. 'How much did you drink last night? Ake Bluefinn! His lords. Their wives and children. His men! A whole shipload of the buggars from Alekka! All here to make an alliance. You know that. It's all Eirik's been talking about for weeks.' He blinked, checking to see that Eadmund wasn't teasing him. 'Didn't you wonder who all those people were in the hall last night?'

Eadmund tried to piece together the images of the night before, but his shoulders slumped at the effort, and he remained sitting on the bed in a defeated heap.

He looked ill, Thorgils thought, even in the dim light of the old cottage. Pasty and bloated. Getting fatter by the day. It was often hard to find a glimmer of the handsome warrior who'd once had the ladies of Oss arm-wrestling to see who would be his wife.

Thorgils grinned, the familiar twinkle firmly back in his eye now. 'The Lord of Blixo has a very pretty daughter,' he said with a wink. 'Don't think Eirik was expecting that. He's had his head together with Hector Berras all morning.'

'Fuck.' Dropping his head to his hands, Eadmund let out a low groan. 'Why doesn't he leave well enough alone? How many times do I have to tell him? I don't want a wife! I don't *need* a wife!'

'Maybe. But you do need someone to give you a bath, so if you don't want a wife, get yourself a nursemaid! Someone to wash your face and wipe your arse, seeing as how you don't appear able to do either by yourself!' Thorgils' red curls shook as he snorted, enjoying the filthy look he got in return. 'Come on, let's get to the Pit before Torstan swims away. It'll keep Eirik off your back to see you doing something more with that arm than pouring ale.' He dragged Eadmund to his feet. His bare feet, he realised, looking around for any sign of a boot as Eadmund staggered before him.

'Anything to keep me out of the hall,' Eadmund grumbled. 'I don't want to bump into this girl, whoever she is.'

Thorgils grinned, throwing a boot for Eadmund to catch. 'You can hide, but on this island, there's nowhere to run, you know that. Not from a twitchy king with a throne to protect! And besides, I've a feeling you wouldn't want to run anywhere if you took a proper look at her. Though, if you're not interested, perhaps I'll have a word and see if our king will do a little matchmaking for me!'

Eadmund ignored Thorgils, dropping his head as he tugged on his boot. It was still wet, and he felt cold, suddenly aware that his cottage was full of holes. That there was no fire. Nothing to eat.

And now his father wanted to play matchmaker.

Again.

He looked up with a sigh, but not in time to avoid the next boot which Thorgils had lobbed at his head.

***

Edela could feel her granddaughter steaming with anger as she took a seat beside her on a log of driftwood that lay across the windswept sand. 'You will not endear yourself to anyone by killing that man.'

Jael's eyes were fixed on the waves, white-capped and rolling with fury, just as she was. She was too angry to even turn towards her grandmother.

Too angry to speak.

'Your temper...' Edela tried. The wind was a howl, and a roar and her voice disappeared into it.

But Jael heard her.

'My temper?' She spun around, glaring at that sweet old face, unable to remove the venom from her voice. 'You want to talk about my temper? You think I killed Gudrum's son because I've got a quick temper? That he did nothing to deserve it?'

'I think Lothar sits on the Brekkan throne, not Axl,' Edela panted, still out of breath after hurrying to catch Jael. 'Not you.' She glanced around, but the cove was deserted, apart from the shipbuilders working on Lothar's new vessels, but they were far away, well out of earshot. It felt like more rain was coming. Always rain lately, which, Edela supposed, was good for her overgrown garden. 'And Lothar will decide what happens next, and only Lothar.'

'He's giving Tig to that bastard!' Jael dropped her head to her hands, scratching her braids, wanting to pull them loose. Trying not to scream. 'Tig! My horse! *My* horse!' She felt sick at the thought of handing him over to Gudrum Killi.

'He is. And you know it wasn't Lothar's idea. That ridiculous lump is not clever,' Edela snorted. 'Is he? Not clever enough to hurt you this much.' She shivered, tucking her cloak under her legs.

Jael softened her scowl, eyes full of pain. 'No, it was Gudrum's idea. His son knew how to hurt me, and he did, killing Asta like that. Everyone knew how I felt about that dog. Gudrum's playing the same game now.' She pushed her boots into the cold sand, annoyed by how vulnerable she felt.

'He is, but you can't let him win, Jael,' Edela said, her hand like ice as it gripped her granddaughter's. 'And he will. If you reveal your pain, they will both win. If you do something foolish, they will both win. It's what they want, can't you see?'

Jael could, but it made little difference. Her breathing slowed, though, her shoulders curling forward. 'But I can't let him take Tig, Grandmother. I won't.'

'You must,' Edela insisted. 'If he doesn't, there will be a terrible price to pay. I've seen it in my dreams, Jael. You must let Gudrum take Tig.'

The waves crashed onto the shore in an angry rhythm, and Jael felt her body crashing with them, not wanting to imagine what Gudrum planned to do to her horse once he got him away from Andala.

***

After escaping a sudden downpour, which had quickly turned into a full-blown storm, Eirik had ushered his guests into the hall. Their turn around the square, browsing the market, had been brief. It wasn't a very big fort, and with the longstanding tensions between the islands and Alekka, traders did not rush across the Akuliina Sea; not if they wanted to stay on the right side of their king, whoever he happened to be. So Oss' market was usually a meagre affair, with few traders arriving to set up their stalls – mostly furs and skins, sometimes soapstone and iron – and Eirik knew that if he wanted to change things, he needed to secure this alliance.

He was determined to let nothing get in the way, though the thought of Hector Berras' lovely daughter had suddenly become an unexpected distraction. He frowned, remembering what Eydis had said about trouble. And anything to do with Eadmund would inevitably end in trouble. But if he didn't find his son a wife soon, what would become of him?

And what would become of his kingdom?

Oss' hall was loud, full of energy and chatter as the Alekkans became more comfortable in the company of their hosts. Eydis could hear the voices humming around her as she perched on her little wooden chair beside her father's throne. The happy noises merged into the roar of wind and rain outside. She could feel bursts of icy cold air as the doors opened and closed, more Osslanders hurrying inside to escape the rapidly worsening weather. Thunder was getting closer, shaking the walls now, and Eydis sunk back into her chair, enjoying the wildness of the storm.

She could hear her father fussing around his guests, apologising for the leaks in the roof, offering them spiced wine, breaded scallops; suggesting they sit closer to the fire. He sounded nervous, she thought, likely wondering what state Eadmund would be in when he arrived.

Knowing that soon he would come, as he always did, looking for ale.

'Hello, Eydis.'

Eydis flinched, recognising that voice.

Evaine Gallas. Morac's sixteen-year-old daughter.

Strikingly beautiful, with long white-blonde hair that tousled in waves down towards a narrow waist. Small and lithe and big-eyed, she looked around the hall, not seeing any sign of Eadmund. 'Your brother is missing again, I see. I hope he's somewhere dry.'

Eydis almost didn't reply, but she could sense that someone was standing beside Evaine, and she didn't want to appear rude. 'Yes, I hope so.'

'Hello, Eydis,' Runa Gallas smiled. 'That storm is awful, isn't it? I wish they'd keep the doors locked. It feels as though the wind's about to tear them off their hinges!'

Evaine turned to her mother with an embarrassed grimace, wishing the old woman away. And though Runa was only middle-aged, in Evaine's youthful eyes, she was a grey-haired, fussing old crone always trying to get in between her and Eadmund, the man Evaine knew she was fated to be with.

She wished Runa would just go away and bother someone else.

44

Eydis smiled. 'I like storms.'

'Do you? Well, I am surprised,' Runa said, ignoring Evaine huffing and puffing beside her. While they were in the hall, with Eirik and his guests present, she felt much more confident around her daughter, knowing that Evaine would not dare do anything to cause trouble. She needed to keep on the right side of Eirik Skalleson if she wanted to marry his son, though Runa secretly hoped that Eirik would never encourage such a match. The thought of Evaine as the next Queen of Oss was a nightmare she didn't want to live through. 'Next, you'll tell me you like the cold too!'

'Well...'

'Runa. Evaine,' Eirik grinned, coming to a stop in front of the dais with three of his guests. 'Have you met the Berras' yet? Lord Hector and his good wife, Cotilde. Their daughter, Orla, too.'

Runa's face, usually tense and anxious, broke into a genuine smile. She was always pleased to meet new people. Oss was a tiny island; a place she had lived her whole life, and though she had no real desire to leave her home behind, new faces were always welcome.

Evaine's nostrils flared with distaste, though she fixed a smile on her face, running her eyes over the girl. Hardly a girl, she thought, trying not to sneer. She looked like a desperate woman, well past her prime, with that gaping, toothy mouth and all that ridiculous orange hair. Not someone Eadmund would look twice at, she was sure. Hardly a woman suited to being the next Queen of Oss.

'I am sorry for the weather,' Runa apologised. 'It won't leave you with the best impression of our island, will it?'

'No, but it will give you an honest one,' Evaine smirked.

Eirik glared at her, not sure why Evaine felt the need to share her opinion about anything. The irritating girl was like a wild horse that Morac had failed to tame. She was quickly becoming a problem he would have to attend to.

But Orla smiled happily. 'I must admit that I like stormy weather. It's quite exciting really, all that wind and rain.'

They looked at her as though she was mad, listening as the

howl of the wind intensified into a painful cry.

Eydis felt puzzled. Her dreams warning her of trouble contrasted sharply with the sweetness she could hear in Orla Berras' voice. She sounded as though she was often smiling. It was confusing, and Eydis started to doubt her dreams again, wondering what use she was to her father at all. Perhaps she was simply imagining everything? Causing him problems by revealing what she saw?

Then the loud bellow of Thorgils Svanter distracted them all as he burst inside, doors banging behind him, shaking rain and sleet from his shaggy hair and furry cloak, stomping his way towards the fire.

Eirik sighed in relief, seeing his bedraggled son standing with him.

Standing was a good start.

He encouraged Orla and her parents towards the fire, realising that he needed to get back to Ake Bluefinn who appeared to be looking around for something to drink. 'I'll go and grab that son of mine and be right back, then I think it will be time for something to eat!'

Evaine turned to follow him, but Runa put a hand on her shoulder, holding her back.

'I don't think the king wants you there,' she said nervously. 'Best we leave them to it.'

Evaine flung Runa's arm away, almost snarling as she headed after Eirik, only to be blocked by Morac, who grabbed her hand and bustled her towards the green curtain that shielded the bedchambers from view.

Once they were safely out of sight, in the torchlit corridor, Morac spun around, peering at his daughter down his long thin nose. His usually sallow face was almost purple with anger. 'You will not cause trouble, Evaine. Not now. Let Eirik have his fun without any interference, do you understand me?' he hissed, watching her face twist and turn as she tried to escape his hold. Glancing up and down the corridor with cold grey eyes, Morac was relieved to see that they were alone. 'You won't help your cause by becoming a problem, will you?'

'And if Eadmund likes this girl?' Evaine panicked. 'What if he does?'

Morac laughed. 'Eadmund? He hasn't liked one of them yet, has he? Why would he start now? And, more to the point, why would she want Eadmund? He's a stinking mess. You were a mere child the last time he held a sword long enough to do damage to anyone except himself. Why would a lord like Hector Berras want his only daughter married to Eadmund?'

'Perhaps because he wants her to be a queen, married to a king, which Eadmund will soon be!' Evaine wasn't convinced by her father's argument, and she was starting to worry that Orla Berras looked more likely than any of Eirik's previous candidates combined. Evaine could feel her heart throbbing in her chest at the thought of Eadmund being tempted by the woman, and, clamping her teeth together, she seethed at her father. 'I will not let anyone have Eadmund, Father. No one! No one can have him but me. You know that!'

Morac was struggling to maintain his patience around his increasingly erratic daughter, though he needed to calm her before Eirik stepped in. 'Go then, but keep your distance,' he warned. 'You won't be able to stop anything if Eirik banishes you from the fort. And we all know that he's capable of it.' Morac eyed Evaine sternly, but she was already brushing stray hairs away from her face, smoothing down her pretty blue dress. And before Morac could open his mouth to say any more, she spun around, flouncing out through the curtain, scanning the hall for Eadmund.

Morac watched her go, shoulder blades tight, the deep crease between his wiry grey eyebrows a jagged cut. Shaking his head, he tried to clear his face of worry as he followed after her.

***

'Lothar's going to have trouble with Jael,' Gudrum murmured, his eyes on the warriors grappling and grunting in the training ring. The ring where he had trained and fought against his friends, his enemies. Ranuf. Gant too. 'Can't see why he let her live. After Ranuf died? What was he thinking? Surely you warned him, old friend?' He glanced at Gant, whose stern face had never given much away. Despite his grey hair, he appeared little changed from when Gudrum had left Andala. He was still lean, his hands calloused from working daily with a sword.

Much like him.

Gant didn't move his head, his eyes seemingly fixed on the battle between two reasonably matched warriors, neither prepared to give in. Boys. Boys like he had been with Gudrum once. Gant had never liked him, but he'd always admired how tough he was in battle. Ranuf had kept him by his side for years, insisting that victories would be easier to come by with skilled warriors working together, whether they liked them or not.

That had been true.

There had been many victories to savour, but the bitter taste of Gudrum's betrayal remained.

'You say that,' Gant muttered. 'But you could have killed Jael. I'm sure Lothar would have considered it. Instead, you chose to take her horse. That's the sort of game-playing that got your family into this mess in the first place.'

Gudrum sucked cold air through cramped teeth. The lice may have left his head, but they now appeared to be living in his beard. The itch was so intense that he wanted to scratch his chin until it bled. But he grunted, shoving his hand down by his side instead, pressing it against the railings they leaned over. 'You think I should kill her for Lothar? Me?'

'You had reason to then. You've reason to now,' Gant suggested coldly. 'And Lothar would thank you. So you choosing not to says you're either afraid that she'd beat an old man like you, or you prefer a little torture to a helping of revenge. Not sure your son would agree either way.' He was working hard not to turn around and punch Gudrum in his smug mouth. 'Think I'd rather my father killed my murderer than played children's games with her.'

'Ha!' Gudrum laughed, ignoring the anger that felt hot as it rushed up his body. Gant Olborn had bettered him more than once over the years. Many times, in fact. Ranuf's favourite. His pet. And now, here he was, betraying Ranuf's children by clinging to Lothar like a desperate barnacle. Old and soon to be irrelevant, Gudrum was sure. 'Seeing as how you didn't know my son well enough to say such a thing, how about we leave it to me to decide the best way to avenge his death.' He snorted, turning his attention back to the fight as the younger of the two men felled his opponent with a powerful hook to the jaw. 'Death is easy. Final. Living with loss... that's what's hard. Losing everyone you love, one by one... that's what's hard. Death is no revenge. Where's the pain in that?'

Gant heard the bleakness in Gudrum's voice, and he turned towards him, but Gudrum's eyes appeared to shrink even further into his hairy face, masking the true meaning of his words.

'Besides,' Gudrum smiled, pushing himself away from the railings as the rain came down with force. 'I need a new horse.'

CHAPTER FOUR

The storm worsened, and nobody left the hall.

Parts of the roof felt as though they were lifting, which worried Eirik who had only just finished having it replaced; though it was obvious now that it hadn't been constructed with much skill or care considering the leaks that were multiplying as rain dripped down into buckets.

The three members of the Berras family didn't appear to notice. Eirik had ensured the kitchen staff remained busy, and the mead girls attentive with their buckets of golden liquid. Though, panicking suddenly, he spun around, searching for Eadmund, worrying how much mead his son had already consumed. He raised his eyebrows at Thorgils who sat at a table, arm wrestling Torstan, which seemed like a pointless exercise, Thorgils' arms being nearly twice the size of his much smaller friend's. Thorgils blinked, losing concentration as Eirik inclined his head towards where Eadmund sat with a group of friends, urging him to go and check on him.

Torstan slammed Thorgils' hand down onto the table to a few hearty cheers, but Thorgils was already on his feet, worried too; he could see Ake Bluefinn eyeing Eadmund curiously.

Pushing his way into the darkest corner of the hall, where flaming torches spluttered through a deluge of leaks, Thorgils found Eadmund leaning on their friend Erland. He was slopping more mead over the side of his cup than he was managing to deliver into his mouth, attempting to tell a joke in between gulps.

Thorgils stopped.

Eadmund looked happy. Almost. And turning around, he could see that Ake had turned away, talking to one of his lords. Thorgils shrugged at Eirik, not seeing any need to intervene. Eirik frowned back, nervous, but he agreed. Best to just wait and see. He could feel himself almost holding his breath, though, too afraid to look away, knowing that Eadmund had ruined everything else he had tried. It was surely inevitable that he would shove this off a cliff too, but... perhaps not?

'Is there somewhere we can go and talk? In private?' Ake wondered from his right. He was a hulking man, though quiet-spoken, with a deep, reassuring voice; a man whose reputation as the greatest warrior Alekka had ever seen appeared not to have gone to his head.

Eirik nodded, leading Ake through the curtain, down the corridor towards the bedchambers. He had another chamber reserved for more private conversations, and turning to the right, he pushed open the door, pleased to see a fire burning. Wind rushed down the smoke hole, rain sizzling the flames, but the room felt almost warm. A jug waited on the table with two of Eirik's finest cups. Bronze, ornately decorated with coiled knots. From Kalmera. A wedding gift for his third wife.

He frowned suddenly, tension rising and falling, trying to leave his worries about Eadmund at the door as he made his way to two chairs placed on opposite sides of a low table. Motioning for Ake to take one, Eirik took the other.

'You have a lovely daughter,' Ake began, grabbing the cup Eirik handed him. Eirik's wine was a delight, flavours he had never tasted before: an odd combination of crowberries and rhubarb that had him intrigued, ready to take a barrel or two back to Stornas with him. 'It makes me wistful for my own. They wanted to come, of course, but they are so young. Perhaps next time, when I shall have one more, or maybe this time, a son?'

The light in the chamber was diffuse, a dull golden glow flickering around the dark room, and Eirik could see the warmth in Ake's eyes. He smiled. 'I wish you luck with that. It's hard to have a daughter, especially a blind one. I worry about her. Spend my time trying to think of how to keep her safe. Though, it's been much easier than having a son!'

Ake smiled, though he did not laugh. He could almost feel the pain in Eirik's words, and though they had been enemies for as long as they had been kings, he did not revel in it. He was a serious man with a hooked nose; short, thinning brown hair and a long, olive-skinned face dotted with stubble. Thick eyebrows sat low over a pair of prominent brown eyes; sometimes full of merriment, often weary. Being a king had sucked the fight out of him.

Ake had been hungry for Alekka's throne as a young man; fought for it for nearly two decades. Through blood and grief and death and pain, he had conquered every enemy, every rival, every faction in Alekka. Made it to the throne alive. And then he'd met his wife, and she had given him two daughters, and now, like Eirik, he lived in a world of worry and problems.

Always fretting about what came next.

Ake ran a hand over his stubble, scratching his cheek as he leaned forward. 'Though we have been enemies, we have more in common than most friends.'

Eirik smiled, sipping his wine, relaxing slightly. 'True.'

'It is better, I think, to have more friends than enemies,' Ake suggested. 'To unite with those you can respect and admire, instead of remaining stuck, clinging to the old ways. Living in the past, holding on to those things which no longer serve us. We need to move towards the future we want to create for our children and their children. A better one than either of us had.'

'I agree,' Eirik nodded. 'What was the point in all we fought for? Just to keep fighting till we die? Not even a moment to savour victory? We claimed thrones with our own blood, yet how little time is there to sit on them and enjoy what we built?'

A bowl of nuts sat on the table, and Ake grabbed a handful, popping two in his mouth. 'Ahhh, now you're just teasing me, Eirik. Sitting and savouring? Don't you mean sitting and listening to moaning, arguing, raving people who all want something from you? Mother and father to them all? Arbiter of every argument? Chooser of every fate? Ha! We may as well be gods!'

They both laughed, enjoying the rare occasion of being able to share the burden with one who knew what it felt like to carry the same cumbersome weight of leadership.

Thunder crashed, and Ake's face was suddenly serious. 'The alliance we forge will be important for both our kingdoms. More important than either of us realises today.'

Eirik had the distinct feeling that Ake had more on his mind than he was prepared to reveal.

'Alekka is a big kingdom. So much land, but spread wide and thin, much of it uninhabitable,' Ake went on. 'My people are growing divided again, ruled by their hate for their neighbours.' He sat back, his bloated belly protruding, embarrassed for a moment that he'd let himself turn into a soft-bellied king. 'My kingdom is held together by the smallest of stitches now. Held together by me. By my reputation. It's all we have, in the end, isn't it? Our reputations. What people believe about us, true or not. And when they stop believing...'

'You sound as though you've seen something coming,' Eirik wondered, draining his cup. 'You have a dreamer?'

Ake froze. He knew Eirik Skalleson's last wife had been a dreamer. A woman he had taken from Tuura, though how Eirik felt about dreamers himself, Ake wasn't sure.

Still, he had to trust someone.

'I do. And she sees trouble coming. Always trouble.'

Eirik shook his head. 'I know how that feels. My dreamer sees the same.'

Ake was surprised by that. He had not seen any dreamers in Oss' fort; none that Eirik had revealed to him at least. 'Well, we are both in the shit, then!' he laughed. 'So we may as well come together. Things will only get worse, won't they? Better to help each other swim through it all.'

Eirik lifted the wine jug, offering it to Ake, enjoying the rich tang of the deep-red liquid warming his chest. 'We may as well,' he agreed, banging his cup into Ake's. 'So tell me, then, what is it that you have in mind?'

***

After her unsatisfying talk with Edela, Jael had left the cove behind, walking further away from the fort, needing to think. She had wanted to head for the stables, take Tig and ride until they couldn't be found, but she couldn't leave her family behind. Lothar dangled them over her like an unspoken threat, glinting eyes always seeking her out when he was talking to Gisila or Edela or Axl. Even Aleksander.

Like a cat considering a mouse.

No matter how playful that cat pretended to be, padding gently with soft paws, its sharp claws were always there, hidden, ready to strike at any moment.

Finally returning to the fort as the afternoon shadows lengthened, Jael was irritated to see Osbert walking towards her, a familiar smirk on his face. Her cousin was an annoying shadow at times, always where she least wanted him to be.

She needed to find Aleksander and work out a plan.

She didn't need to deal with Osbert.

The rain showers of earlier in the day had given way to a luminous blue sky and a late summer warmth, and as Jael hurried around Osbert, she almost felt like removing her cloak.

'Gudrum will leave tomorrow morning!' Osbert called after her, seeing that Jael had no intention of stopping to talk with him.

And then, Jael did stop.

She spun around, glaring at her cousin who straightened his spine as he approached. His face was freshly shaven, his pale-brown hair combed until most of the kinks had been smoothed away. He had even changed his trousers, though now he felt irritated that he'd bothered. Jael was staring at him as though he was shit stuck to the bottom of her boot.

As usual.

'What do you want, Osbert?' Jael sighed, opening up her hands in confusion. 'A smile? Conversation? Coins?' And shaking her head, she turned away, heading across the square, ignoring the whispers and the looks that followed her, and her own feelings of terror that a maniac like Gudrum Killi was about to ride off with her horse.

Sweeping his cloak around, Osbert hurried after her. 'I'm not after anything, Cousin. Just thought you'd like to know. In case you wanted to say goodbye.'

Jael stopped again, spinning around, hearing the barely-concealed glee in his voice. 'And you think that will get me into your bed, do you? Playing games? You think *that's* the best strategy to get what you want from me?' She stepped forward, leaning over her shorter cousin. '*Hurting* me? You think you're *hurting* me?'

Osbert stepped back, jutting out his chin. 'I think you get what you deserve, Jael. When you reject opportunities for a better life, you get what you deserve. If you'd made a different choice, I could have protected you. Protected your horse. My father would have listened to me.'

'What?' Jael could see her mother coming towards her with Osbert's younger sister, Amma, and the worried expression on Gisila's face checked her anger somewhat. There was more than just her own fate to consider, she knew. They had all lost a lot when Lothar had stolen the throne, but none more so than Gisila who had gone from being the Queen of Brekka, living in the comfortable King's Hall, to sharing a dark and tiny rundown cottage with her son and a servant. 'You think you have some sway over your father? That he cares what *you* think about anything?'

'I'm his closest advisor!' Osbert insisted, puffing out his chest, though he immediately doubted his own words. Lothar was fickle. Changeable. Some days it was as though they ruled together. Other times he worried that his father was going to have him killed.

'You're his only son, so he endures you,' Jael said, reading the doubt in Osbert's eyes. 'If it doesn't serve his interests, he won't listen to you. Surely you know that? You must see how things will go?'

'Jael!' Gisila exclaimed, panic stripping her voice of any strength as she forced her way into the conversation. Her smile was tight, and her sunken dark eyes were blinking rapidly, worrying that her fiery daughter was about to cause trouble. She'd heard what Lothar had done with her horse, and she didn't want Jael to make things even worse, for surely it could get worse? 'Aleksander was looking for you. He was outside the armourer's. Something about a new shield?'

Jael could see the fear in her mother's eyes, and she took a breath, nodding. 'Alright. I was just wasting my time here anyway. Lothar wouldn't listen to you even if I was your wife, Osbert.' She shivered, not wanting to imagine that horrific fate. 'When are you going to see the truth?'

Osbert was too busy frowning at Jael to notice the smile on his sixteen-year-old sister's pretty face as she dropped her eyes, hiding her lips behind a hand.

'I'll walk with you,' Gisila insisted with a quick nod to Amma, not wanting to be left alone with Osbert.

Jael didn't hear her as she stormed off, desperate to get away from her cousin before she made things even worse by punching him in the mouth.

***

They had talked for long enough for Ake and Eirik to realise how much sense it made to formalise an alliance. One that would benefit both kingdoms, and give them the promise of help from their neighbours across the Akuliina Sea in times of trouble. For both kings, and their dreamers could feel trouble coming.

But then there was the problem of who would come after them.

'My wife is with child. My dreamer believes she will have a son.' Ake's grin brightened his face. He felt a surge of pride and excitement. Terror too. Estrella had lost two babies trying to give him a son, and he worried about both her and his unborn child. Though his dreamer had seen that the boy would arrive in the winter, his shoulders remained permanently frozen with tension, hoping the old woman was right.

Eirik's eyes were bright, though a little blurry after so many cups of his strongest wine. 'That is something to celebrate for sure!'

'It is, and it gives me hope for my kingdom. I would not want to leave it in the hands of my daughters and whatever husbands the boys they are promised to turn out to be. How could I trust them to do what is right? To do what I would have done?' He swallowed, not wanting to imagine his little girls as married women. They were only eight and nine. Too young for such talk.

'You have a long time to hang on, then!' Eirik joked, his blue eyes bursting open. Then his face fell. 'My son is...' He didn't know where to begin.

'He needs a wife!' Ake slurred, spilling wine on his red tunic. 'Every man needs a good wife. Women bring out the best in us. Good women, with clever heads on broad shoulders. He needs a wife!'

'I've been trying, believe me,' Eirik groaned, his back aching now. The temperature was plummeting, the shrinking flames not enough to keep the chamber warm. He could feel a cold draft rushing under the door, more wind creeping in through holes in the walls, fluttering the tapestries. And reaching for the woodpile, he threw another log onto the flames. 'Eadmund is not as open to the idea as I am.'

'Then you must give him no choice!' Ake insisted. 'Which is why I brought Hector along with me. His daughter too. She is a fine woman, wouldn't you say? Hector is my closest friend, my most loyal lord, and his daughter is smart and kind, the sort of steady hand your son appears to need in his life. She would make a good wife, a good queen, I'm sure. It is worth considering. A way to further strengthen our ties.'

Eirik grimaced, caught somewhere between joy and pain. He lifted his shoulders, straightening his aching back. 'I... she is certainly striking to look at.'

'She is. But also generous and sweet. Funny too. My wife spends a lot of time with Orla, and she considers her highly. In fact, it was her idea. A way to unite our two kingdoms.'

'And... she would be... open to it?'

'Hector has let himself be guided by her. She's found no one to capture her interest yet, so we shall have to see. But don't worry, I imagine the thought of becoming a queen one day will be impossible to resist, despite any... problems your son may have.'

Hearing a loud crash from the hall, Eirik swallowed. Likely Eadmund, he thought, wondering how eager Hector Berras and his daughter would feel once Eadmund fully revealed what a mess he was. 'We should get back to the hall. I would like to see my son, talk to him about things. Or, at least, try to sober him up.'

Ake laughed, wobbling to his feet. 'Yes, we have a long night ahead of us, I'm sure. If your son can last that long!'

***

Jael and Gisila reached the armourer's without an argument, but that was mainly because Jael was so tense that she couldn't even peel her lips apart. Tense and conscious of the need to keep her thoughts to herself. Gisila had become fretful and frail since her husband's death. Lothar hounded her, and she pacified him, hoping to keep her children safe, out of his clutches. Any hint that Jael would step out of the shadows and cause trouble had Gisila panicking.

As she was now.

'I'm sure Edela would appreciate a visit,' Jael suggested, hoping to send her muttering mother on her way. She glanced at Aleksander, looking for his support.

'I'm sure she would,' Gisila said tartly, stumbling back as two yapping dogs chased each other around the armourer's hut, one of them getting sent on its way with a sharp kick that had Jael frowning. 'And I will go and see her, but before I do, you must know that Gudrum Killi is not a man to play games with.' Her voice was a whisper, and Jael stepped closer, grabbing her mother's arm.

'Why do you say that?'

Gisila glanced around, tucking her long dark hair behind her ears, tired of the wind tangling it in her mouth. 'After you killed Ronal, Gudrum was... understanding,' she began. 'He seemed to accept Ranuf's decision that there would be no repercussions, no blood price. But it was just for show. Gudrum was only biding his time, waiting to take revenge.'

Jael was surprised to hear that. She blinked at Aleksander who looked just as shocked. 'What did he do?'

'Plotted to kill you. He *was* plotting, with his friend, that one-armed man, what was his name...'

'Bilic?' Aleksander suggested, old memories stirring of the time when they were training to be warriors, both of them looking up to Ranuf and his close circle of men, Gudrum and Bilic included.

'That's right, Bilic.' Gisila shuddered, lowering her voice even further, her eyes always moving. Into the armourer's hut. Down the muddy path lined with lopsided wattle fences, smoke pumping all around them from the worksheds lining the path. The armourer was next to the blacksmith, next to the silversmith, next to the tanner. The combined stink of all that bone-coal, urine, dung, and smoke was eye-wateringly unbearable. 'Gudrum had it all planned out, how he would ambush you, kill you, make it look like it was raiding Islanders sent by Eirik Skalleson. We would have believed it, wouldn't we?'

Jael's mouth hung open. Her father had never told her.

'But what happened?' Aleksander wondered.

'Bilic couldn't go through with it. He couldn't betray Ranuf like that, so he confessed all. Ranuf had men searching for Gudrum. Gant was there. Oleg, I remember. But Gudrum had already left for the safety of Iskavall. Welcomed by Lothar and Hugo Vandaal. Ranuf brought it up, of course, when he visited Ollsvik, but Gudrum denied it, and Hugo, with Lothar in his ear, wouldn't go against him. Then Bilic died mysteriously not long after, so there was no one left who -' She stopped suddenly, smiling as Lothar appeared around the corner. 'Lothar!'

Jael and Aleksander froze as their king waddled into view, cloak flapping behind him.

Lothar's fractious mood brightened at the sight of Gisila, and he smoothed down his black moustache, licking his lips, stopping close by her side. 'Getting weapons made, Gisila?' he joked, nudging his shoulder into hers. 'Hoping to come along with us to see to the Hestians?'

Jael thought she might vomit, watching as her mother transformed her anxious frown into a pleasing smile.

'No, not for me,' Gisila laughed. 'I would hardly know what to do with anything more dangerous than a brooch pin.'

Lothar patted her arm, standing even closer. 'Which is exactly how it should be, my dear.' He eyed Jael. 'We don't want a kingdom full of sword-wielding women like your daughter here, do we? Who would do all the menial chores? Who would keep the men happy in their beds?'

Aleksander bit his tongue. No matter how much they all wanted to fight back against Lothar, they knew there was little point in causing trouble. Their future rested on the smallest of certainties. One tiny step in the wrong direction, and who knew what Lothar would do.

Jael didn't bite hers.

She was finding it increasingly hard to keep herself together at all. Some days the fire building inside her was easily controlled; she could clamp her lips together and maintain a dull-eyed look. Other days the burning heat proved too much to contain. 'I've never had any complaints,' she muttered, jaw clenched.

Recognising the look on her daughter's face, Gisila hurried to distract Lothar who had already stiffened in response. 'The market looks busy this morning,' she smiled. 'You must be pleased to see so many traders in the harbour. I saw a lot of ivory and so many furs. I must find something to warm up my cottage before winter arrives.' She was mumbling about nothing that mattered, but it did serve to distract Lothar, whose attention was quickly on Gisila's deliciously pink lips.

She looked tired, he thought, but still more desirable than any woman in Andala. 'Well, why don't I walk you down there and we'll see what we can find. I'm sure they would be more than happy to supply their best furs to the king.'

Gisila nodded, slipping away before either Lothar or Jael could say another word.

And lifting a hand to his simmering niece and her almost-holding-his-breath lover, Lothar followed after her.

***

Thorgils grabbed Eadmund by the collar of his tunic, trying to get his friend to focus as he eased him down onto the bench. 'Eirik will be back soon, and he's going to find a dribbling mess unless you sit up!' He was too uptight to have touched more than a few cups of ale, knowing that Eirik had left him in charge of Eadmund, and after too much mead, his friend was predictably starting to lose control of himself.

Eadmund kept seeing the girl with the flaming orange hair everywhere he turned, and her presence was agitating him. She was hard to miss, and he felt embarrassed seeing the pity in her sparkling blue eyes when she turned them on him. They were so bright, like the sky on that rare day on Oss when it wasn't grey or raining, snowing or blowing a gale. That one perfect day of pure blue, cloudless sky.

Eadmund blinked, trying to right himself, though his body, lacking any muscle now after years wasted in the pursuit of ale and women, made no effort to do what he wanted. It slumped over the table like a pile of sloppy mud. His hazel eyes were defeated as he turned them up to his friend. 'Maybe water?'

Thorgils looked surprised, but he hopped away to find

Eadmund a cup of water, banging into Eirik who had returned with Ake Bluefinn, both of them unsteady on their feet now; broad grins on flushed faces. 'Sorry!' he exclaimed, hoping his king was too drunk to notice Eadmund's predictable demise.

Eirik did notice, but encouraged by his talk with Ake, he ploughed forward, taking a seat next to his son, hoping to sober him up. Grabbing the cup out of Thorgils' hand, he sniffed it before smiling in approval and handing it to Eadmund. 'This will help. A few of these and we'll go for a walk.'

'In this weather?'

Rain was dripping somewhere behind them, falling down the smoke hole, splashing the flames, running in under the hall doors.

Everything was quickly becoming a soggy mess.

'It's just what you need,' Eirik insisted, a smile on his face as he watched Orla Berras talking with her attentive mother. 'That wind will wake you up, I'm sure.'

Eadmund wasn't, but sensing everyone's eyes on him, he sipped the water and tried to still the sway of his body, nodding mutely, tired of feeling like a useless fool.

CHAPTER FIVE

After arriving back at their cottage, Jael and Aleksander had encouraged Biddy to go and visit Edela, much to her annoyance. Biddy was always pleased to visit Edela, but not so pleased to think that Jael and Aleksander didn't want her to hear what they were planning.

It worried her as she trudged away from the cottage into a sudden downpour, carrying a plate of smoked sausages and cheese. A few figs too. She knew how much Edela liked a fig.

Jael shut the door, feeling it wobble loosely in her hand. They would have to replace it before winter, she thought distractedly, turning to Aleksander who sat on their narrow bed with a frown.

'You can't take Tig,' Aleksander sighed. 'I can't take Tig.'

'No, Edela's right,' Jael agreed. 'We have to let Gudrum leave with him.'

That didn't sit right with either of them.

'So, we follow him?'

Jael nodded, joining Aleksander on the bed, pressing her body against his, her lips near his ear. Lothar had spies in the fort, though she still wasn't certain she knew who they all were. Greed was a weakness often not revealed in a character until it was tested. And Lothar, though his coffers were emptying fast, was not afraid to spend his gold and silver coins on getting what he so desperately wanted, which was a way to get rid of her. Lothar Furyck may have been a king, but as powerful as that made him, he was always at risk of losing support if he made a move to oust his niece and nephew. He had to tread carefully, and that made him vulnerable. 'You should follow Gudrum,' Jael whispered. 'Lothar will expect me to do something. Or maybe he won't, but Osbert certainly will. That sneaky little shit will be watching. And Tiras.'

'Well, Tiras is always watching.'

'They may be watching you.' Jael frowned, wondering if that was true. Sometimes she could sense things so clearly. Other times it was all a muddy blur. 'I'll do something to keep their attention here, on me.'

Aleksander leaned back, staring into her eyes. 'What sort of something?'

'I don't know. Gudrum will have taken my horse, so they'll be expecting me to cause a fuss. Lothar will be hoping for it, so it would be strange if I didn't react.' She blinked as another idea came to mind. 'Unless I try to distract Osbert instead?'

'No.' Aleksander didn't like that idea. 'You're a terrible liar.'

Jael couldn't even smile, but it was true. 'Osbert said Gudrum's leaving in the morning. I asked around, and apparently, he's going to join his men in Orlstad. His ship is there. They'll be sailing to Stornas.'

'And he'll just have the men he came with? The rest have gone from Ollsvik?'

Jael nodded, her hand on his leg. It kept twitching; unusual for a calm man like Aleksander. 'But even so, you can't go alone.'

'There's only five of them. Best we keep it simple.'

She glared at him. 'You can't go alone.'

Aleksander nodded reluctantly. He didn't doubt that Gudrum had brought his hardest men to Andala with him, anticipating trouble. Despite his round cheeks and a hint of a belly, Gudrum still looked made of iron; they could both see that. 'I'll ask Jonas. He's always keen for some trouble, especially since Malin died.'

Jael glared at him some more.

'Alright, Isaak too.'

'Three against five?' She felt tense, wanting to be the one who ripped out Gudrum Killi's throat; not wanting to risk anyone else getting hurt for her, or her horse. 'Might be enough.'

'It will be,' Aleksander assured her. 'I'll get Tig back. I'll put Gudrum in the ground.' He squeezed her hand. 'I will. I promise.'

Jael thought about her father, wondering what he would do. She didn't have to wonder for long. His voice roared in her ears. 'Kill the bastard,' he urged. 'You have to kill him, Jael.'

And smiling, Jael kissed Aleksander. 'Be careful. You're never as good as you think you are. Remember that.'

Aleksander laughed, his eyes quickly turning sad. He missed the way it used to be: Ranuf and Gant, him and Jael, riding off to battle at the head of the Brekkan army. 'Haven't heard that in a long time.'

'No, me neither, but no matter what we think of Gant anymore, it holds true. Don't think you can beat Gudrum easily. He's good at games, at fooling people. Remember what Gisila said? Don't let him outthink you.'

Aleksander nodded, wanting to get back to the kissing. 'Biddy should be gone for a while,' he murmured, his hand roaming up Jael's thigh.

'She will,' Jael agreed. 'So we've plenty of time to go and find Jonas and Isaak. See if we can get them on board.'

Aleksander frowned as she slid away from him, readjusting her swordbelt with a wink as she headed for the door.

***

Winter was coming.

Eirik stood before the hall doors, enjoying the bitter whip of the wind as it slapped his leathery face. He had managed to drag Eadmund outside with him for a time, and despite no obvious signs that his son had listened to him, he had seemed slightly more sober when he'd escaped back inside.

Eirik shivered, his mind alert now as he surveyed the storm-battered square. Most items had been packed away. The braziers, benches, and tables remained, abandoned, but the traders and their stalls were gone, all the livestock secured back into their sheds. There wasn't a person in sight. Eirik squinted, realising that that wasn't true, lifting a hand to Entorp Bray who struggled towards him, into the wind, thick fur cloak billowing like a sail in a squall. 'You're a bit late!' he laughed as Entorp tried to get his cloak under control. 'Think the food's almost gone in there. We started early today!' He clapped Entorp on the back, surprised when he sneezed.

Entorp didn't look bothered by the thought of missing out on the food as he wiped his nose with a cloth he'd tucked into his trousers. 'I promised Eydis I'd come. We're going to talk about herbs.'

'Oh, well, she wouldn't want to miss that,' Eirik snorted, though Entorp didn't notice as he hurried past his king. He was a serious man, odd-looking, with a shock of tufted orange hair, and tiny bones braided into his orange-and-white beard, but a good man nonetheless. A wise man, Eirik realised, grabbing his arm. 'Wait, Entorp, what do you think about the chances of Eadmund ever finding a wife? A good wife? I've had no luck matchmaking, I know, but perhaps, finally, I've found the right woman.' Despite the ear-splitting wail of the wind, he heard a cheer from inside the hall, and he cringed, hoping that Thorgils had a tight rein on Eadmund. 'Perhaps.'

Despite his warm cloak, Entorp shivered, thinking that this wasn't the sort of conversation to have outside in a storm. He sighed, deciding that to walk delicately around the ice lake of truth would only give him frostbite. 'Eadmund will not marry willingly, my lord. I think it, and so does Eydis, and she sees more clearly than all of us put together. You wish to find a solution to a problem, I know, but Eadmund is a man of heart. His is still broken, even now. And only he, I believe, can repair it. Eadmund and the right woman.' Entorp snatched at his cloak again as it flapped around him. 'The right woman at the right moment. When the gods will it. Those who are old, those who are new. They all believe that fate comes for us when it is time. We are not the masters of our destiny, no matter how much we wish to believe it isn't so.'

Eirik let go of Entorp's arm, nodding slowly as the old man threw back the hood of his cloak and entered the hall. He saw the burst of orange light, smelled the stink of smoke and ale, heard the bellow of greeting, and sighing, Eirik turned after Entorp, more confused than ever.

***

Evaine didn't like the way Eadmund was looking at Orla Berras. Nor the way Orla Berras was looking at Eadmund. They were talking across the hall, standing by one of the thick carved posts that held up the leaking roof. Eadmund was leaning against it, obviously trying to hold himself up too.

Evaine could see that.

It was as though she knew everything about him. As though she could see inside his head, feel his pain. She was the only one who knew how to help him. If only she could get him away from the hall, back to his cottage where they could be alone.

She could see how it was all expected to unfold.

Alliances were always tied to marriages, and a marriage for Eadmund was all Eirik had cared about for years. He was wasting his time, though, Evaine knew. There was only one woman Eadmund was meant to be with, and it wasn't that orange-haired wretch he was standing next to.

Evaine shifted her gaze away from Eadmund to where Orla's parents watched from the high table where they sat with the King of Alekka, all three of them nodding their heads, murmuring to each other in satisfied tones.

Feeling herself panic, and not bothering to say goodbye to her mother or father, Evaine hurried for her cloak, slipping out of the hall.

Eadmund looked up as a burst of cold air blasted inside,

wondering who kept opening the doors. But, he realised, he was just trying to distract himself. He had been pushed into this conversation, and he'd spent the entire time trying to devise a plan of escape.

Despite that, Eadmund couldn't deny that Orla was easy to talk to. She seemed kind and welcoming, brushing past everything that felt awkward with a soft voice that had no edge to it. It was not a demanding voice, nor a playful one. She had a sense of humour and lightness about her, but she seemed content just to talk. It had almost been pleasant for a time, but now Eadmund desperately wanted ale, and his leg was shaking in irritation as he debated how quickly he could find some without looking either rude or desperate. But then he would catch himself drawn back to Orla as she laughed, her freckled nose wrinkling, teeth showing. She didn't appear to be making an effort, and it confused him.

He didn't want to like her at all.

He didn't want a wife, but if he had to have one... if his father was never going to give up until he gave in...

Eydis, sitting nearby, listening with interest, was frowning.

'Not sure why you're in such a bad mood,' her father laughed, plonking himself down onto his throne, leaning over to kiss her cheek. 'You who love your brother more than anyone. He seems happy over there. Or perhaps you've forgotten what that sounds like?' Eirik's eyes drifted away from his daughter to where Ake was watching with Hector and Cotilde Berras. He nodded his approval and Eirik sat back with a grin. 'He does look happy, Eydis. You can smile about that, I promise.'

But Eydis' frown didn't budge. 'There's a cloud, Father,' she whispered, knowing that Morac was likely lurking about, listening. He always was. Eydis didn't like him, nor did she trust him, though she would never reveal her thoughts about that to her father. Eirik's loyalty to Morac was not something she would attempt to pry loose. Not yet.

'What cloud?' Eirik was barely listening now. He smelled roast salmon, and licking his lips, he turned to see trays being carried out of the kitchen, which was just as well as Ake had started to look a little hungry again. 'What do you mean, a cloud? It's a storm, Eydis, there are many clouds!' He laughed, though his daughter's serious face quickly sobered him, and he leaned towards her, sensing her reluctance to speak plainly.

'I don't know, Father. My dreams are hard to understand most of the time, without any training...'

Eirik pressed his lips together, not saying any more. He knew what Eydis wanted, but he had no intention of giving it to her.

'But when I see Orla Berras and her family, I see a cloud over them. A dark cloud, sinking low. I don't have a good feeling. She will cause trouble.'

'*Orla?*' That wasn't what Eirik wanted to hear, and looking at the sweet girl, it made no sense at all. He shifted his eyes to Eadmund who was glancing around, no doubt searching for something stronger than water. 'If only you could see what I can,' he tried to convince his daughter. 'You would change your mind, Eydis, I know you would. I'm not sure I've ever met a woman more perfectly suited to your brother. It's as though this was meant to be.'

Thunder crashed overhead, and Eydis clamped her lips together. She could hear more than anyone: every lie, every unspoken wish, every desperate fear.

She could hear more than anyone, and she could hear how much her father wanted something to change with Eadmund. They both did. But there was no joy to be found in shoving a large boulder into a tiny hole.

A tiny hole made for a very specific, special stone.

And Eydis felt with all her heart that Orla Berras would never be that stone.

***

The night was cold, but Jael and Aleksander enjoyed the chance to escape the furtive eyes of gossiping Andalans as they slowly walked back to their cottage. Clouds hid the moon, so it couldn't watch them either.

It felt as though they were entirely alone.

Aleksander put an arm around Jael's shoulder, and she leaned into him, surprising them both. 'You must be very cold!' he laughed, though she didn't appear to be shivering.

Jael ignored him. She was always cold. It wasn't that.

She just felt odd.

They didn't leave the fort without each other. Not for a fight. Not ever.

'You need to be careful,' she warned. 'Think things through. You don't always see everything coming.'

'Oh really?' Aleksander lifted an eyebrow. 'Never heard you say that before.'

'Well, I've always been there, keeping you out of trouble.'

'Is that so? Thought it was the other way around?' He laughed, feeling odd himself. 'You can't come, so there's no point worrying. I'll get Tig back. And then we'll think of a way to...' Aleksander stopped, realising that someone was probably lurking in the shadows.

Likely Tiras.

Jael could sense what he'd been about to say. She was quiet, thinking about Lothar. About her father. About how sad it was that her home had become such a torturous place to be now; all her memories of her father ruined by Lothar. His presence tainting everything.

She didn't want to stay.

But where would they go? And how could she walk away from Brekka?

Though her father had not wanted her on the throne...

Aleksander squeezed her arm as they turned the corner, seeing the familiar silhouette of their horrible little cottage in the distance. He turned Jael to him, holding her close, his lips by her ear. 'We'll get rid of Lothar, I promise. He won't sit on that throne forever. It's Axl's throne, and one day, somehow, we'll take it back. Together.'

***

Eadmund felt so tired that he'd been tempted to sleep in his old bed, in his old chamber in the hall, but remembering that his father had put the Berras family in there, he'd headed back to his cottage, stumbling between Thorgils and Torstan who were well used to helping Eadmund walk.

'Eirik looked pleased,' Thorgils grinned, easing Eadmund down onto the bed while Torstan tried to secure the cottage door. 'With you.'

'Makes a change!' Torstan laughed, sweeping his burning torch around the cottage, noticing the ash heap in the fire pit. 'I'll get you some wood. You're going to need something to keep you warm tonight without the lovely Orla in your bed!'

Eadmund frowned, wrapping his cloak around himself. 'There's plenty of wood,' he slurred, not even able to see a hand in front of his face, nor the white puffs of breath smoke blowing before him in the cold shack. 'You go. I'm fine.'

'Fine to fall asleep and freeze to death,' Thorgils snorted. 'And what would our king do to us then? Leaving you to die just before you married the woman of your dreams!'

Eadmund's frown intensified. He gripped his head, trying to stop it moving. 'She's not the woman of my dreams,' he said dully.

Thorgils stopped smiling. 'I know, I know, but maybe she'll make you happy? Wouldn't be so bad to be happy, would it? After all these years? I bet you'd like to be happy again?'

Torstan headed for the door, not wanting to be stopped. He would get the wood, and they would make Eadmund's cottage warm enough to see him through the stormy night. They had been friends since they were swaddled babies. Eadmund would do anything for him, he knew, as he would in return.

Eadmund didn't answer Thorgils, but his mind wandered back to Orla.

She was funny.

He remembered how easily she had laughed. How comfortable

and confident she appeared. Not bothered by the dripping roof or his drunken state.

And guilt swelled up in his chest as he turned towards the pillow, wanting to go to sleep. Not even the call of ale was as urgent then as the desire to sink into a dream. He didn't want to think about Orla anymore.

He wanted to disappear.

'Well, you lie down there,' Thorgils chuckled as Eadmund toppled over, cloak on, boots on, eyes closed as soon as his head hit the pillow. 'I'll help Torstan get the fire going, then we'll leave you to it.' He stared at his friend, not smiling now, trying to remember the man he had once been. But lifting the tattered fur over Eadmund's back, he realised that he no longer could.

***

Evaine couldn't sleep.

Her bed, on the mezzanine, was the most comfortable in her father's luxurious house. Morac had done well for himself as Eirik Skalleson's closest advisor over the years. The Gallas' home was the finest on the island, and Morac had ensured that Evaine had her own space, far away from him and Runa, who enjoyed the privacy of the downstairs bedchamber.

It suited Evaine as well. She could head down the stairs and out the door without ever alerting her parents to her plans. The stairs creaked, as did the floorboards, but the storm was so violent overhead that Evaine couldn't even hear the sound of her father's thunderous snoring as she secured her cloak to one shoulder with a large bronze brooch. Both her parents snored, oblivious to any other noises in the house, and Evaine was grateful for it, especially on a night such as this.

She turned the key with a look back into the darkness, relieved to see nothing but the faint shadows of flames flickering across her parents' bedchamber door.

And lifting her hood over her hair, Evaine slipped out into the night.

***

Gudrum had drunk nearly everyone under the table, yet he still looked keen for more.

Lothar was finally ready for his bed, though he had enjoyed his evening enormously. Andala felt like less of a home than Ollsvik had ever been. Despite being his father's second, much less favoured son, he had tried to fight Ranuf for the Brekkan throne after their father's death. He'd had little support, though, and against Ranuf's strength and experience, no chance. Lothar had been younger, weaker, poorer. Not a very good warrior. Disliked by many. Dismissed by even more.

He had failed and been banished to Iskavall as a result.

A mistake, he thought, with a wry grin.

His brother's mistake had been to leave a challenger to his throne alive, and Lothar had never stopped thinking about it, knowing that one day a chance would come his way. So he collected loyal men and wealth, drawing himself closer and closer to Hugo Vandaal; becoming an invaluable aide in that snake pit of a kingdom; helping to keep Hugo's many enemies at bay.

And being paid handsomely to do so.

By the time Ranuf died, Lothar was in the perfect position to take what he had so desperately sought for all those years.

And he had.

Quickly and decisively, he'd disrupted Axl's ascent to his father's throne; spreading rumours, undermining his viability; infecting the whole of Brekka with lies and fears about how useless a boy Axl Furyck truly was. How dangerous it would be to the stability of the kingdom to be ruled by one so inexperienced. What with the growing threat posed by the Islanders? The Hestians?

No, what they needed was a man. An experienced man.

A Furyck.

And time had moved on, so that many had forgotten what a sneak Lothar had been. A sneak and a leech. A greedy man of such weak character that he had tried to overthrow his own brother, going against their father's very clear wishes.

They had forgotten perhaps or forgiven, because it was better to have a king who could save them from the enemies they feared, than one who would make them feel vulnerable and weak.

The people of Andala had looked to Jael, but Ranuf had sidelined her, which had shocked her as much as it had them. And a sidelined Jael had surprisingly sat back and let it happen.

Lothar wondered why. Again.

What was she planning?

And why was he letting her live to find out?

'Are you sure you'd rather ride off on that horse than fight it out with my niece?' Lothar mumbled between yawns. 'It would help us both if you took her life as the blood price. It would certainly help me.'

'Perhaps Gudrum doesn't think he could beat Jael?' Osbert slurred from his father's left. 'Perhaps he thinks killing her horse would be easier?'

Gudrum's smile remained on his face, his hands around his cup of ale, but as he looked past Lothar to his son, his eyes hardened like a cooling bar of iron. 'You may fear that woman, Osbert, but I don't. I could kill her, but I want to *hurt* her. Just like your father here does. He's a smart man. He sees how much more pain he can extract from his enemies by forcing them to witness his success.' Gudrum's eyes were gleaming again. 'You need to think, Osbert. One day the throne will be yours if you use your head, and learn when to hold your tongue. And it's always better to hold your tongue around experienced men. Men skilled enough to cut it out.'

Osbert leaned forward, his eyes sharp in the darkening hall. He looked to his father to defend him, but Lothar only nodded in agreement, distracted by the sudden absence of wine.

'Gudrum's right. Foolish kings with flapping tongues don't last long. Just ask every king who's sat on Iskavall's miserable throne. All those years I was in Ollsvik, Hugo was safe, protected. And the moment I leave?' Lothar tried to snap his fingers, but they were sweaty, and there were too many rings squeezed onto them, so they made no sound. Ignoring that he peered at Osbert, trying to focus, though his son kept blurring before him. 'Jael may see herself as free, but she's our prisoner. Our prisoner who we torture every day just by keeping her alive. Here. Where the memories of her precious father torment her every time she steps into this hall. Every time she fights in the training ring. Gudrum's right,' Lothar decided suddenly. 'He's doing the right thing.'

And just like that, Lothar convinced himself once again that leaving Jael alive was the best path to take. The one that would see him emerge as an even more powerful king in the long run.

A king who knew how to crush his enemies with their own pathetic weaknesses.

***

Eadmund wanted to resist.

He'd tried.

But Evaine kept coming back, slipping into his cottage, and she was so persuasive with those pouting lips and eager hands of hers.

Tonight, though, Eadmund felt odd. He tried to push her away as she crept into his bed, naked. He tried to insist that he was tired. That his father would be furious. That he had to get up early.

His excuses fell away, though, as Evaine's hands slipped under the fur and her warm body writhed against his, heating his frozen limbs. The fire Torstan and Thorgils had made hours earlier had not been able to withstand the assault of wind and rain, and it had gone out quickly, so Eadmund had woken with teeth chattering when the door creaked open.

It was hard to resist a warm body on a cold night.

'I won't stay long,' Evaine breathed, kissing Eadmund's cheek, trailing her lips down to his mouth, inhaling the delicious earthy scent of him. 'I just felt so lonely. I missed you.'

Eadmund was weak, with tiredness, with ale. With unhappiness most of all. He'd tried desperately to dream of the past, though nothing would come except thoughts of orange-haired Orla and the future. Thoughts he didn't welcome, not believing he could ever be happy again.

But Evaine...

Evaine was like a cup of ale. A temporary feeling of pleasure that took away the darkness, just for a while. Just long enough for him to see a flash of hope.

Turning to her, Eadmund pushed her hair away from her face, bringing her close, feeling her legs wrap around him, trying to ignore the familiar voice in his head warning him away.

CHAPTER SIX

Eirik felt younger than he had in years as he walked down the beach, across the slick black stones, holding Eydis' mittened hand. The storm had gone and the morning was almost bright, with a hint of sun glowing behind a bank of light-grey clouds. Waves pounded the stone spires guarding the harbour in the distance, and the cries of sea birds were loud as they called down from their nests in the jagged cliffs surrounding Oss' harbour.

He turned around to look at his guests who were further back, walking together, not as certain on the challenging surface. He'd wanted to give them a chance to talk alone before they sat down to discuss the possibilities of more than just an alliance.

Nerves jangling suddenly, Eirik wondered if he was doing the right thing, feeling Eydis' hand in his, knowing that she was convinced that he was certainly not doing the right thing. He glanced back at Ake, who smiled, lifting a hand as if to reassure his host that all was well.

Ake Bluefinn liked Oss.

It surprised him.

Surprised him how much he liked Eirik Skalleson too. It was odd to discover that he had more in common with his enemy than some of the men who'd been by his side for years. That they shared a common purpose, and a deep devotion to their families. Not all men felt the same, he knew. Some saw wealth and power as their motivating force. Perhaps he had too, when he was young and starving, much like Eirik, who he knew had been raised a slave by his brutish father, Grim, once the master slave trader of the entire northern realm.

And now, there was Grim's son, gently guiding his blind daughter across the black stones as though she was more precious than all the gold in the world. Which she was, Ake knew, thinking about his own girls, eager to get home to them. To see how his wife, Estrella, was feeling. She had been ill when he left, though she'd assured him that it was perfectly normal.

Still, he wanted to get home. He always felt better when he was in his hall, sitting on his throne.

Turning to Hector, Ake caught sight of Orla and Eadmund walking further back, both of them slightly more awkward around each other in the very cold light of day. Ake smiled, shivering. 'What do you think, then? Would Orla like to live on such a block of ice?' His eyes were back over his shoulder again, making a pretence of fussing with his hooded cloak, but really he wanted to see how comfortable Orla looked. She was like a daughter to him, and despite his confidence in her, he didn't want to push her towards an unhappy fate. 'Would she welcome a husband like Eadmund Skalleson? He is perhaps not quite what you might have wished for...' Ake's voice was low, checking how far Eirik was ahead of them, though the noise of the sea roaring in the distance, and the screech of the hungry birds, was enough to drown out even a shouting man, he was sure.

Hector looked hesitant. 'He has some... problems,' he muttered with a frown. 'More than I realised. Cotilde isn't happy. She's fretting. Though we both know that Orla is strong enough to cope with whatever life throws at her.'

'Of course she is,' Ake assured him. 'And she does like the cold from memory.'

'Ha! She does,' Hector agreed, remembering their trips up north to The Murk when she was just a girl. That wild place remained blanketed in snow all year round. A dark, ominous world of warring tribes, and certainly not the safest place to take a child, but the best hunting ground he'd ever visited. Brimming with elk, deer, bears; polar bears too. If it had been easily accessible by ship, he would have trekked up there every summer. 'Though there's more than snow to contend with here, isn't there? And if Eadmund doesn't get... better?' Hector sighed, his face falling, the sun finally emerging from behind its prison of clouds, shining down on his bald head. 'I'm responsible for her choices. For helping her to make the right ones.'

'You're a better father than most, my friend,' Ake said. 'Few would look past what they would get in return. A daughter who will one day be a queen? The benefits that will come from our alliance? The gold? Few would care past that.' Ake felt a chill on his head, wishing he'd brought his fur hat with him. He glanced at Hector, who didn't seem bothered by the cold at all. 'You should look at Orla. She seems happy.'

Hector turned around as Orla slipped. He made a move to hurry to her, but Eadmund grabbed her first, and although his daughter appeared far steadier on her feet than her companion, Hector started to relax. 'Yes, she does,' he conceded, watching Orla's eyes twinkle in the sunshine. She was an unfailingly honest woman, he knew. He would have noticed if it was all forced politeness. He had tried to marry her off once before, and that man had barely elicited a smile from her.

No, Ake was right, Orla did seem happy. But for how long?

'These stones take a bit of getting used to,' Orla smiled at Eadmund, worried that her nose was running down her face. Everything felt so numb and cold that she couldn't tell. She dug beneath her furry cloak, searching for her purse.

Eadmund tried to smile. Guilt had hung over him like a snow cloud as he dressed and headed to the hall for breakfast, knowing that his father would send Thorgils to collect him if he didn't show his face. Evaine had come and gone so quickly in the night that he was starting to believe he'd dreamed it. Whatever the case, he had to fix the lock on his cottage door. She was just a girl. She needed to find someone her own age.

He blinked, realising that Orla was talking to him. 'I'm sorry?'

'Your sister. Eydis. I was just wondering if she had always

been blind?' Her eyes were full of sympathy as she kept a firm hold of Eadmund's arm.

Eadmund nodded, worried that he was about to topple over and take Orla with him. He felt as though he was at sea, rising and falling with the waves. He needed to sit down quickly. 'Yes... she was born blind, though it's never stopped her. She's just as determined as anyone. Sometimes I wonder how she gets around so easily, but I suppose she knows every part of the fort by now. Eirik worries about her constantly. I imagine that's what fathers do.' His eyes were on Hector Berras before him. The man couldn't stop turning around, and Eadmund found himself sweating uncomfortably, wanting to unpin his cloak.

He was suddenly so thirsty.

'They do, especially mine.' Orla peered at her father, hoping he would stop worrying. Eadmund seemed like a good man. A man who needed help. He had such sad eyes and a gentleness about him that she felt drawn to. He was almost shy, embarrassed as he walked with her. It made her relax, and she found her mind wandering to what it might be like to live on Oss.

Eadmund didn't say anything else, and eventually, Orla turned to him, noticing how flushed his cheeks were. Despite the frigid morning, he appeared to be sweating. 'Shall we sit down?' she suggested, spying a bench in the distance. 'I think I need a break.'

Eadmund knew she felt sorry for him, but he didn't care. He was starting to shake. He needed to sit down before he fell down. He had to pull himself together.

Watching from the top of the muddy hill that led down to the beach, Evaine felt her body tense, rage boiling just beneath the surface. 'What are we going to do?' she hissed, turning to glare at her father. 'What?! It's different, isn't it? *This*. I can feel it, Father! There is something about that woman! What are we going to do?'

Morac didn't feel as concerned as Evaine. If Eadmund were to marry Orla Berras, it would not be the worst thing that could happen. But one look at his daughter's face, and he realised that it would potentially be the worst thing that could happen to him.

He would never hear the end of it.

Sighing, Morac put an arm around Evaine's shoulder. 'Why don't we go back to the house? It won't help you to stand here watching. Eirik won't like it.'

But Evaine wasn't even listening as she wriggled away from her father's arm, charging back through the gates before he'd even turned around.

***

Tig was still in the stables.

Gudrum and Lothar had been awake for most of the night drinking, and Jael was pleased to have some time to spend with her horse before Gudrum took him away.

She blew out a breath, not feeling confident in their plan.

And if Aleksander did get Tig back, how where they going to explain it to Lothar, who would undoubtedly recognise the horse after all the fuss that had been made in the square. Or would he?

He would, Jael knew, shaking her head. Lothar was foolish but not stupid, or blind. Though it didn't matter. They would figure something out. Aleksander just had to bring him back first.

Tig whinnied loudly, knocking his head against hers. He thought she'd come to take him for a ride, yet all she had done was stand there feeding him treats and sniffing.

Jael could tell that he was getting impatient and she smiled. It was never good to form an attachment to an animal, she knew, but she had. Tig had been by her side for fourteen years. He was a fighter, trained to kill. They'd been going into battle together since she was eighteen-years-old.

He was strong. Fiery. Bad-tempered.

Just like her.

She couldn't lose him to a vengeful bastard like Gudrum Killi.

'You seem to be feeding *my* horse treats he doesn't deserve,' came the rasp of a voice that made Jael cringe. 'It's not a good habit to encourage in a beast. Softness. Thinking rewards come for no work. I prefer a well-trained horse. One who works hard and expects nothing.' Gudrum hung over the door to Tig's stall, an arrogant smirk puffing up his round cheeks.

It reminded Jael of his son, Ronal, and she shivered.

'I didn't see the harm in saying goodbye,' Jael muttered, trying to avoid those eyes that were so eagerly seeking out the pain in hers. Though perhaps it would encourage Gudrum to think that nothing was amiss if he saw how broken-hearted she was? 'You want to deprive me of that too?'

'And did you give me a chance to say goodbye to my boy? Did you stop before the final blow? Stop and think, wait, I should find Gudrum, let him come, say goodbye before I stab Ronal through the heart?' He bit his yellow teeth together, still trying to keep that smile going, but the snarl in his voice was thick with intent now.

Jael stepped towards him. 'You want me to say I'm sorry, but why would I do that when I'm not sorry at all.'

'*Still?*' Gudrum was surprised. 'When I'm taking your precious horse? You're not sorry enough to beg me to stop? Plead with me to leave him behind?' He licked his lips, running his eyes over Jael's breasts, though there was nothing much to see there, he knew. 'My son made a mistake. It was a boy's mistake, and it deserved a boy's punishment, yet you killed him for it. And now, all these years later, you're too arrogant to admit it? You can't admit that you were wrong? That given another chance, you'd do it differently?'

Jael could smell fresh manure. Steaming, warm, fresh manure. She could hear men in the stables saddling their horses; someone complaining as they mucked out a stall. And she tried to think clearly, not wanting to make it all worse.

Aleksander was right, though, she was terrible at lying.

But not only terrible at lying, she found it impossible not to say what she really thought, even in the most precarious of situations.

'I'm not sure I would,' Jael admitted, staring Gudrum down. 'Your son was sixteen. That's no boy. He knew what he was doing. And he knew who he was doing it to. He fought me enough times to know what I was capable of. You know it too, which is why you're choosing a horse over a fight. You know I'd kill you.' She saw Gudrum flinch, bunched-up cheeks puffing up further, broken veins bright red across his crooked nose.

Gudrum lunged forward, eyes afire. 'You think you can make me fight you, bitch? Prove myself to you? You think I need to do that? Against you? Ha!' He stood back, quickly getting himself under control, straightening his tunic, adjusting his swordbelt, needing to use his hands to do something other than squeeze the life out of her. 'Your father didn't think much of you. For all his talk, he left you with nothing but a sword. Your uncle thinks nothing of you. And no one came to support you when Ranuf died, when the throne was up for grabs, did they? No one. Not one of Ranuf's men came to support you, so why do you think you're so unstoppable, Jael Furyck? So powerful? So masterful? That you could defeat me? *You*?'

The reminder of what had happened after her father's death was still a fresh wound, and Jael could feel her right hand twitching, her chest a building storm, sharp pains darting in from every side. 'How will we ever know if you're too cowardly to find out, Gudrum? Not even to avenge your son? Not even for that?'

Gudrum stepped back again. He could see the anger in those green eyes everyone found so mesmerising. Green eyes with just a hint of gold, he thought, as he turned and walked away.

Eyes full of anger.

And fear.

He smiled, looking over his shoulder. 'I'll go and see your king, then I shall come for my horse. Say all the goodbyes you like, little girl, it won't be long now.'

Jael watched him go, gripping the hilt of her father's sword, her heart racing. Swallowing, she turned around to Tig, hoping she hadn't just made everything even worse.

***

Orla sensed that Eadmund wanted to leave.

He couldn't stand still. His legs kept shaking. He blinked at her, trying to keep his smile going but it wobbled, just as he was wobbling before her.

The weather had brightened even further, and after their walk along the beach, Eirik had suggested that Eadmund show her around the fort.

Eadmund had felt almost relaxed, at first, but though the old stone fort was not large, it was taking some time to wind their way down the small back alleys, around the rows of tiny cottages cramped so tightly together that Orla was certain the Osslanders would be able to hear their neighbour's whispers. Nearly one thousand people were squeezed into those homes, leaving the rest of the fort to house the big hall and the even bigger square, with room for two guard towers and several stables; outbuildings, sheds and stalls, barns too.

There was a lot to see, and Orla wasn't unhappy with what she saw, despite the mud and her increasingly twitchy companion. 'Would you like to go back to the hall?' she wondered gently. 'I could do with something to eat. I keep thinking about the whitefish your father served last night. I've never had it raw before. It was so tender.' It wasn't really true, and she would have been happy to continue on for some time. She'd never had much of an appetite, but she wanted Eadmund to relax.

Eadmund nodded, leading the way, feeling as though he was being jabbed by hundreds of tiny icicles. He couldn't even speak. He needed ale.

More than anything, he needed ale.

And then Evaine was there, eyes aflame at the sight of Eadmund with that woman. But she forced a smile, working hard to ignore him. 'Your father was looking for you,' she mumbled to Orla, struggling to make eye contact. 'He sent his servants to find you.'

Eadmund straightened up, pleased to have another reason to get back to the hall quickly. He blinked at Evaine, hurrying Orla away from her, not thinking about ale for a moment.

Entorp stood watching them from across the square, Eydis

beside him. 'It's Evaine,' he whispered, answering her unspoken question. 'Causing trouble again, no doubt. That girl will not take her claws out of Eadmund without a fight. She seems to believe that he belongs to her.'

Eydis could feel the warm fur of one of Entorp's white cats as it curled itself around her stockinged legs. Entorp's cats acted like loyal dogs, always following him on his errands, and they were especially fond of Eydis. 'Well, if my father has his way, she won't think that for long. Not if he marries Eadmund to Orla Berras.'

Entorp lifted a boot out of the mud, shaking it before continuing their journey to the gardens which he had planted on the more sheltered side of the fort. They were going to pick herbs to make a tea, if any had survived the wild night. Entorp had taught Eydis' mother everything she knew about herbs and symbols, and he knew that Rada would have wanted her daughter to have the same knowledge, despite what Eirik thought about Tuuran dreamers.

'And you don't like the idea of that?' Entorp wondered lightly, not surprised that Eydis had reservations too. 'She seems like a lovely girl from all appearances. Always smiling.'

'But she's not the right one, is she?' Eydis asked softly. It was something she felt deep inside. 'She's not the right one, Entorp.'

'No, she isn't,' Entorp agreed. 'But I doubt anyone will listen to us, will they?' He hurried Eydis along, not wanting to get stopped by Evaine who always made a habit of trying to befriend Eydis, hoping it would help her in her quest to claim Eadmund's heart.

But Evaine Gallas was not the right woman either.

Entorp knew that for certain.

***

'Where are you going?' Osbert wondered, gnawing on a toothpick. He eyed Aleksander suspiciously. Aleksander Lehr, his rival for Jael's affections.

He frowned, knowing that wasn't true.

His cousin hated everything about him. There was no competition for her affections at all; Aleksander had won that battle years ago.

But still, he didn't like the man.

One of Brekka's finest warriors, or so he'd been told since the day they'd arrived.

And his father had not wanted to part with a warrior of that skill and reputation, not with the battles he had planned.

Osbert was under orders to leave Aleksander alone.

Aleksander felt an odd flutter of panic stir in his limbs, sensing Osbert's eyes trying to seek out everything he was trying to conceal. Gripping the reins of his horse loosely in one hand, he indicated with his chin to the bow slung over his back, and to his two heavily armed companions on horses behind him. 'Hunting. What does it look like?'

Osbert wasn't easily convinced. 'Why now?'

Aleksander tried to look bored, though his entire body was humming with urgency. 'What do you mean, why now? I go hunting all the time. The weather's fine, so we're going hunting.'

Osbert frowned. 'Without Jael?'

'Jael's saying goodbye to Tig. And the rest is none of your damn business,' Aleksander growled. 'What we talk about is not yours to know, Osbert.' He quickly latched onto the only idea that would appeal to Jael's slimy cousin: that they'd had a fight.

And right on cue, Osbert's snivelly face brightened. 'Well, fair enough,' he said, stepping away from Aleksander's horse. 'Go hunt. I'm sure Jael will find someone else t   o comfort her.' And smiling at Aleksander, he turned away, wondering how long Gudrum was going to be.

Aleksander's shoulders dropped in relief as he nodded to Jonas and Isaak, both of whom looked pleased to see the back of Osbert who was quickly striding off in the opposite direction. And nudging their horses forward, the three men made for the main gates, hoping the rain would hold off.

It was going to be a long day.

CHAPTER SEVEN

After her run-in with Gudrum in the stables, Jael had hoped to disappear until he left Andala, but Osbert found her in Edela's garden, and he was only too happy to inform her that Lothar wanted her to come and say goodbye to her horse.

Jael wanted to scream as she usually did when faced with her cousin, but Gisila and Edela were there, and she felt her mother's panic rise as the silence lengthened.

Edela stepped in. 'She can't.' She knew that Jael had already said her goodbyes to Tig, and she didn't want Lothar to torture her any further for his own sick pleasure. 'I'm afraid you'll have to tell your father that Jael can't. She is unwell.'

'Unwell?' Osbert looked both concerned and suspicious. He stared at Jael who stood in the garden in her faded blue tunic, dark, mud-splattered trousers, swordbelt slung low, scowl on her face. She was quite a sight to behold, he thought. Such a powerful looking woman. So in need of a strong man who could... He blinked, trying to stay focused. 'She doesn't look unwell to me. Perhaps you would like to come and explain to my father exactly what she is unwell with, Edela?'

'Of course, I would be happy to,' Edela announced cheerfully. 'Once I have tended to my granddaughter, of course.' She shooed Jael up the path to her tiny cottage, which sat up a small rise that appeared to be steepening as Edela got older. 'Woman's troubles,' she whispered to Osbert. 'Jael suffers badly. I'd be happy to come and tell your father and his guest all about it if you like, once I give Jael this tea I'm preparing. It will help with the pain, and all that *blood*.' Edela shook her head, looking worried. 'If you'd like to wait there, I won't be long. You can escort me.'

Osbert cringed. 'I... no, no, no need to do that, I'm sure. My father will... he'll understand!' And stepping back, Osbert turned and scurried away from Edela Saeveld and her keen blue eyes.

Edela spun around and winked at her daughter, who stood beside her looking just as confused as Osbert, but happy to see him go. 'Come along, Gisila,' she smiled. 'I've a feeling Jael is going to need this tea to calm her down. Though, we may need to lock the door!'

***

The news that Jael wasn't coming disappointed Lothar, but Osbert appeared quite convinced that she was indisposed, so he didn't pry further. He didn't want to give Gudrum the idea that he had no control over his niece, though he was well aware that he was quickly losing his grip on her and that family of hers. Blinking away his irritation, he turned to Gudrum with a genuine smile. 'I look forward to hearing of your exploits,' he said, watching with concern as Gudrum tried to steady Jael's enormous horse, who skittered angrily, big eyes rolling, black tail flicking with displeasure. He didn't look as though he was about to behave, much like his *previous* owner. 'And an invitation. We can become allies!'

'Are we not already allies, Lothar Furyck?' Gudrum grinned, his voice booming around the square. He was not surprised that Jael wasn't there, but no doubt she was around somewhere, watching as he rode away with her horse, fretting about what he was going to do to the wild beast.

Making a small loop from the end of the reins, Gudrum

slapped Tig on the cheek.

Gant, who was standing beside Oleg, another of Lothar's men who had once been Ranuf's men, cringed, closing his eyes. He knew Tig better than most, and he knew that moody horse would not take it well.

And he didn't.

Rearing up with a roar, Tig flicked his hooves in the air, trying to bring them down on Gudrum's head. But Gudrum was quicker. He knew horses well enough to anticipate what would happen next – especially with a horse that temperamental – and in a battle of wills, it was always better to lay down a marker early. There could be only one winner, one master. And if this horse was going to live and be useful, he was going to have to bend to his new master's will.

And quickly.

Lothar stumbled backwards, flicking a jewelled finger in the direction of Tig, who wasn't about to be slapped again as he danced around, kicking and stomping in a real fury. 'Do something!' he growled at Gant. 'You know the animal! Do something!'

But Gudrum didn't need Gant's help. He threw himself forward, grabbing the reins as they flapped through the air, digging his boots into the ground, holding on as Tig threw himself around, trying to escape his hold. Gudrum was even stronger than he looked, though, and, eventually, Tig ran out of steam, keeping his hooves on the ground long enough for Gudrum to get a boot in a stirrup and haul himself up into his saddle.

Muted cheers reverberated around the square, but there was little interest in what was going on without Jael there.

'Well, now that you've finished showing off, you should get on your way before you end up on your hairy arse!' Lothar laughed as Gudrum's men mounted their horses behind their lord, waiting while he fought to get control of Tig, who was even angrier now that the slapper was sitting on top of him.

Lothar didn't care, though, his attention had already returned to the hall, inclining his head for Gant and Oleg to accompany him. There was an attack to plan, and this time, Lothar was not prepared to be repelled so easily by Haaron Dragos and his sons. He smiled, lifted his fine cloak out of the mud, and headed for the hall, knowing that wherever Jael was and whatever she was doing, she was going to be utterly miserable.

***

Eadmund should have been in the hall.

He should have stopped after two cups.

Now he couldn't count how many cups of ale he'd had, but Thorgils could.

'Too many!' he grumbled, taking a seat opposite Eadmund, a piping hot meat-stick in one hand, a big chunk already missing from it. 'If your father comes out and sees you, he's going to send the lovely Orla straight back to Alekka, isn't he? And then how will you ever get a tribe of orange-haired babies to chase around?'

Eadmund wasn't drunk enough to think that that sounded like a welcome prospect.

'What do you think you're doing, then?' Thorgils wondered, helping himself to Eadmund's cup, getting a grumble in return. 'Turning away every good thing that comes your way? Every chance to climb out of that dark hole of yours? Orla seems like the perfect woman. Imagine what will happen if you spurn her? Mess this up? Eirik won't give up, will he? He needs heirs for his throne. You might end up with a wife like Odda!' Thorgils laughed, though just the thought of his mother made him shiver, and he glanced around the square, hoping she wasn't within earshot. Odda Svanter was a dried-up shrew of a woman who had given birth to a generous giant of a son. It made little sense to either of them, but there it was. You couldn't pick your family, but you could pick your wife, and Eadmund looked ready to ruin another chance to make himself happy. Thorgils gobbled down the last of his hot meat which burned his throat and had him reaching for

Eadmund's cup again, though this time Eadmund was faster and he snatched it away.

'My father's dead,' Thorgils said. 'And Odda doesn't want me to find a wife. Who would chop her wood and light her fires and bring her ale? She has no interest in me being happy, or anyone else for that matter, but you?' He grinned, though his eyes were sad. 'You do. Take the chance. Two kings and one lord are trying to help a shit like you. Let them, Eadmund. Take the chance!'

Eadmund threw back the last drop of ale, ready to raise his hand to Ketil to bring him some more.

But he didn't.

'Alright,' he grumbled reluctantly. 'Alright.' And pushing himself up from the bench, Eadmund stumbled, turning towards the hall.

Thorgils jumped to his feet. 'Perhaps we should throw you into the sea first? Wake you up a bit? You don't want to fall on the poor girl. She'll never marry you then!'

But Eadmund was already well on his way to the hall, determined to stop himself thinking about anything, past, present, or future. He was just going to do what they all wanted. All of them. His father, his friends. They'd all tried to change him, to help him. He needed to stop being a burden to them, a waste of their time. He would do what they wanted.

He would go along with all of it.

He would marry Orla Berras.

***

'I had a dream about you,' Edela smiled, enjoying the comfort of her fur-lined chair. It felt warm and soft against her aching back. She eyed her granddaughter, who stood by the door, wanting to leave. Gisila had already left, worried that Lothar would be suspicious of where they all were; as if they were plotting against him.

Jael rolled her eyes and remained where she was. 'What dream?' she wondered dully, her mind on Tig.

If Gudrum hurt him...

Turning around with a sigh, she came to take the small stool before her grandmother, enjoying the waves of heat from the flames Edela held her hands to. Her grandmother's hands were always so cold, almost black and blue, as though no blood flowed through them. She often wore gloves, even in the summer. And though it was summer, Jael found herself shivering, worrying about Tig again.

And Aleksander.

'You were riding Tig into battle,' Edela began. 'I've not often seen you in battle before.'

Jael was alert, listening.

'You had a bow slung across your back, I remember. You lifted it over your head and shot an arrow into a group of warriors. There was a whole mess of fighting. Gant was there. I saw him. Others I didn't recognise. Some I did.' Edela wrinkled her nose, trying to bring the vision to life again, but it faded, and she slumped further back, tired.

Jael frowned, not wanting to think about Gant. 'What are you trying to say? I've done that before. Perhaps it's not a vision of the future. Just a memory of the past?'

'Axl was there. I saw him beside you.'

Jael stilled. 'Axl?'

Edela smiled, happy to have raised a look of hope on that miserable face she knew so well. 'Yes, Axl, so don't be too worried yet. He's never even been in a battle before, has he, so it was definitely a vision of the future.'

'Did you see Aleksander?' Jael wondered suddenly, edging forward, jumping as the fire popped. 'Did you see Aleksander in your dream?'

'Why?' Edela asked, feeling a cold hand grip her throat. 'Jael? What have you done?'

***

There was one road to Orlstad, and Aleksander knew that Gudrum and his men would take it. Unless Gudrum had lied to Lothar? Unless the whole thing had been an act? It was impossible to know what was true, Aleksander realised as he rode alongside Jonas and Isaak, trying to decide where to stop. The three of them had been arguing about it since they'd left the fort behind. They had to stop somewhere far enough away from Andala not to draw any attention to themselves; far enough away so that Gudrum and his men would have started to relax, but close enough so they could get Tig back home without too much trouble.

And for that, they were going to need to be near a village.

There was one that might work, Aleksander thought, as he urged his horse on, knowing that they would need to get much further ahead to set up the ambush.

They would have to hurry.

***

Evaine had forced herself back to the house, wanting to be alone. Needing to think. Prospective brides had been brought to Oss for years. Young, not so young, odd-looking, attractive, small, plump. All sorts of girls had been ferried to Oss by fathers who wanted to marry their daughter to the next King of the Slave Islands, yet Evaine had not feared that any would claim Eadmund's heart.

Until now.

An alliance with the King of Alekka and a marriage with the daughter of that king's best friend was hardly something Eirik would let Eadmund walk away from. Not in the same way that he'd dismissed the daughters of merchants and traders and lords of insignificant settlements. Island lords too.

But this girl?

Evaine felt sick as she opened up the creaking lid of her wooden chest. No one was in the house, not even the servant who was outside milking the goats. But Evaine still felt the need to hurry as she dug about in the chest, looking for a box. It was small, wooden, symbols scrawled all over it, and finally finding it hidden beneath an old fur wrap, Evaine lifted it out of the chest, feeling her heart quicken.

***

Eadmund had returned to the hall, and Eirik was almost stunned into silence. His son had obviously been drinking. He didn't smell the best. He didn't look the best either: stains on his tunic, straggly copper beard wet with ale.

But he had turned up. Willingly.

And that was something.

Ake looked on encouragingly, and even Hector Berras beside him appeared pleased to see how well Orla and Eadmund were getting on as they stood around the fire with Thorgils and Torstan.

Eirik frowned at Thorgils, hoping he wasn't telling embarrassing stories about Eadmund, which, he realised, he likely was. Thorgils had a big mouth to match his big body and his big head, and Eirik was just about to stand up and try to get his attention when he felt a hand on his shoulder.

Hector.

'We will leave in the morning,' Hector announced. 'My king wishes to get back to his wife. And now that your alliance will be formalised at tonight's feast, nothing is keeping us here.' Hector felt nervous, his eyes meeting his wife's. She looked just as anxious, but one glance at his beautiful daughter and he could see how comfortable she appeared. How easily she fit into the fort. She would make a good queen one day, he knew. And there was nowhere else she would have an opportunity to become one. Nowhere this close to Stornas at least. 'So I would like to discuss our children,' Hector went on. 'Whether you think there is any chance to propose a... marriage? I'm sure such a marriage between our families will only help to strengthen the alliance between the islands and Alekka.'

Eirik tried not to nod as eagerly as he wanted to. He felt like a child at Vesta, giddy with anticipation for that special day that only came once a year. He glanced nervously at Eadmund, hoping he was still half sober; at Orla who was looking at his son as though he was a prize, not a wreck of a once-great warrior. A man who had lost every ounce of respect for himself. Who had given up hope. Who had surrendered his heart to love, and never wanted to touch that hot flame again.

And yet, he would, Eirik knew.

For him.

'Yes,' Eirik smiled, eyes meeting his son's before he turned around to Hector. 'Let us discuss the possibilities.'

CHAPTER EIGHT

Eydis had gone back to her chamber to escape the noise and had promptly fallen asleep. She had not been sleeping well for weeks. Her dreams teased her, and she woke up confused, trying to remember them, hoping to understand what they meant. Most were too confusing to piece together at all. But she was still eager to have them, hoping that, eventually, all the pieces of the puzzle she was being shown would start slotting together, making sense.

As soon as her eyes closed, she saw the woman again.

Eydis had been seeing her for weeks, but she was no closer to discovering who she was or why she kept appearing in her dreams.

And then, suddenly, it all made sense.

This time, the woman was in the square, sitting outside Ketil's with Thorgils and Eadmund. Eadmund looked so different. Eydis couldn't remember seeing him that way before, but, of course, he must have looked that lean and muscular when he was a warrior, before...

The woman was scowling, but her eyes were full of laughter. And then she did laugh, pretending to punch Thorgils. He wrapped an arm around her throat, squeezing, and the woman wriggled away, laughing some more.

Dogs barked around their feet, yapping at a cat who was rolling on its back in the mucky ground nearby, teasing them. Eadmund told them off, but they kept barking anyway, skipping around but never approaching the cat. Too scared by the looks of it.

Eydis blinked, realising that she had drifted away, and when she looked back to the table, she saw that Thorgils had gone, and now Eadmund was leaning towards the woman, grabbing her hand. She snatched it away at first, eventually letting him hold it and he smiled, pleased.

Happy.

Eydis could feel it, like a glowing warmth inside her chest.

Eadmund was happy.

***

Aleksander was not happy.

They'd waited for hours in the bushes, beginning to worry that they'd been tricked.

'Perhaps he's gone back to the fort?' Jonas yawned, picking his nose. 'Perhaps he never left? Maybe there was a problem?'

Aleksander frowned, annoyed to have his fears uttered out loud. His confidence was starting to crumble, his worries multiplying like clouds in a threatening sky. If Gudrum had tricked them, what was he planning?

They were hiding near the road, in a dense thicket that backed onto a wood, just before a river, which meant that Gudrum and his men would hesitate. They would have to. The summer had been a wet one, and the river was sitting unusually high. They would need to approach it carefully.

And that would give Aleksander and his men an opening.

If they weren't being tricked.

He started counting, knowing that soon it would be dusk, and a decision would have to be made before then. Aleksander reached out, patting his chestnut mare who was getting as impatient as he was. 'Ssshhh,' he murmured. 'Just a little longer. Hold on now, just a little longer.'

***

Despite barrels of his father's best wine being rolled into the hall, Eadmund wanted to run.

He eyed the curtain Eirik and Hector had disappeared behind some time before.

'You can do it,' Thorgils laughed, draping an arm over his friend's shoulder. 'Stay awhile longer. See it through. Won't be so bad having a wife. Eirik might give you a new house. Better than that shit cottage you've been hiding out in for years. And Orla will certainly make a better wife than Evaine Gallas.'

'Ssshhh,' Eadmund hissed. 'What are you doing bringing her name up here?' He glanced around as Morac and Sevrin, the head of Eirik's army, approached. 'Evaine is...'

'Yes?' Thorgils dropped his arm, standing so his back was facing the approaching men, wanting to hear what Eadmund said before they arrived.

'None of your business.'

Thorgils looked disappointed, but he spun around with a grin. 'They're serving the swordfish! Swordfish and Kalmeran wine! Our king has saved the best till last, though I don't know how I'll get through it after the last few days.' He patted his stomach, which felt ready to pop.

Sevrin snorted. 'You? You think you'll have problems?' He was as old as Eirik, as old as Morac, though Sevrin's shoulder-length hair was still mostly black. He had a cheerful face, ruddy cheeks, long arms still powerful with muscle; the complete opposite of the gaunt, dour man who stood beside him, nibbling on his thin lips. 'I've known you your whole life, Thorgils Svanter, and I've never seen a bowl of food you couldn't down in the blink of an eye!'

Eadmund laughed, reminded of how true that was. Good memories came flooding back, which surprised him. He tried not to think about the past these days. Not his past at least. 'You do have a reputation to protect,' he insisted, trying to look serious as he eyed Thorgils. 'You don't want those Alekkans to go back home and tell the tale of mealy-mouthed Thorgils Svanter, appetite of a gnat.'

Thorgils' bushy red eyebrows met in the middle of his broad forehead. 'Appetite of a gnat?' he snorted loudly, causing a few Alekkan heads to spin in his direction. 'Well, only one way to silence talk like that!' And he strode off towards the nearest table, looking for somewhere to begin.

Sevrin eyed Eadmund with concern, noting the sweat dampening his curly hair. 'Having second thoughts, are we?'

Eadmund looked cross. 'About?'

'Marriage,' Sevrin grinned. 'It's not for everyone, is it?' He nudged Morac, trying to coax a smile out of that insipid face.

'Don't look at me,' Morac said indignantly, nose in the air. 'I've always been very happy with Runa, and she with me.'

Sevrin could see Runa in the distance, trying to keep Evaine under control. She appeared to be fading away, more miserable than ever, and who could blame her with Morac for company? 'Well, here's hoping Eadmund is just as lucky with his new bride,' he said diplomatically, raising his cup.

Eadmund felt odd, heat rushing up his body. He tugged on his collar. 'Think I might get some air,' he mumbled, turning for the doors.

'Eadmund!'

Eadmund spun in surprise as his sister made her way through the Alekkans and Osslanders who were eyeing the plentiful trays of swordfish and smoked gull eggs being squeezed onto the already heaving tables. 'Thought you were asleep,' he grinned as she grabbed his arm, thinking that his little sister did, in fact, still look half asleep.

Eydis pulled him towards her. 'I need to go outside with you, Eadmund. I need to talk to you. I've had a dream!'

***

The sun was likely going down. It was hard to tell because the clouds had turned a threatening shade of grey, clumping together, making it impossible to tell where the sun actually was.

Aleksander and his friends had hidden in the bushes all afternoon, waiting. And now dusk was likely on its way, and despite Gudrum being a man brimming with confidence, he would surely see the wisdom in not crossing a river you risked getting stranded in as darkness fell.

He would surely have stopped to make camp for the night.

'He's not coming.' Jonas was the more twitchy of Aleksander's two friends. There was barely any fat on his long frame, or any nails on the fingers he was constantly nibbling. He could throw a spear further than any man Aleksander knew of, though. Those lanky arms were surprisingly powerful.

But in the deep gloom of the afternoon, there was no one to throw a spear at.

No one at all.

It was so oddly quiet. The birds could obviously sense that a storm was coming. And then a boom of thunder sounded in the distance.

Aleksander's horse skittered noisily in the leaf litter, not liking the sound of that.

'It doesn't hurt to wait a while longer,' Isaak muttered. He did his talking with an axe, rarely smiling, but he was the perfect man beside you in a fight. Quick and small, with sharp eyes, his speed and skill making him a constant threat. 'Though I could do with a piss.'

Then a sound.

Aleksander put a dirty finger to his lips, head swivelling as he tried to determine what it was.

All three of them froze, shoulders rising, backs stiffening, hands hovering near weapons.

Aleksander blinked at Isaak who nodded back at him.

Horses.

They could definitely hear horses.

***

Jael had left Edela behind in an oddly fretful state. Aleksander had been raised by her parents, her grandmother, and Biddy since he was ten-years-old, and they all worried about him as though he was one of the family. Which he was.

And her fretting had now started to gnaw away at Jael.

Her grandmother was a Tuuran dreamer, and she should have felt that Aleksander was safe. The fact that she didn't was as worrying as the smell of smoke in a dry forest.

'I expect it will take you some time to find a new horse,' Lothar smirked, walking towards her with Gisila who quickly wiped the smile off her face, dropping her eyes, not wanting to see the disapproval in her daughter's.

Jael glared at her anyway, ignoring her uncle.

'And you will need to, Niece. We will be launching another assault on Hest within weeks. I want to keep those Dragos' on their toes!'

Jael blinked in surprise. 'Another assault?' She looked confused. The Kingdom of Hest was carved out of rocks, hidden behind heart-stopping sheer cliffs, accessible only by narrow paths. It was not a kingdom vulnerable to attack. 'Hest?'

'Oh yes, Hest! Haaron's jewel of the South! Soon to be mine!' Lothar grinned at Gisila who smiled back encouragingly, irritating her daughter even further. 'You and Aleksander can come to the hall tonight and *hear* our plans.' Lothar's grin stretched across his bloated face. He never tired of rubbing in the fact that Jael was no longer one of the leaders of the Brekkan army. That her opinion was not required by him, though he knew it should be.

He just couldn't bring himself to ask.

'Ahhh, Aleksander's gone hunting,' Jael said, trying to sound casual. 'I will come, though, if you wish.'

'Hunting?' Gisila's smile was gone, replaced by a look of worry. Happily, Lothar seemed oblivious, though, as he slipped her hand through his arm and squeezed. Gisila tried not to flinch, the sour smell of his sweat suddenly strong.

'Well, do see that *you* are there,' Lothar huffed, turning Gisila away. 'I must show you the latest addition to our fleet, my dear. A fine warship. The biggest in Osterland, I'm sure. One of the many I'm building to conquer the South. Perhaps you can help me name her?'

Jael watched them go, too distracted to feel irritated by her uncle or her mother's pandering for long. The sun was sinking in the sky, heading for the rampart wall, and Jael swallowed, wondering if it had happened yet.

Hoping that Aleksander and Tig were safe.

***

The four men rode past them at a steady pace, heading for the river.

Aleksander, Jonas, and Isaak had chosen new horses, and helmets with full cheek plates and long nose guards. Their cloaks were hooded and plain. They carried no symbols or banners. There was nothing to distinguish them from any other bandit out looking to steal himself some booty, Aleksander hoped, as his spear took the lead rider down.

Isaak's spear hissed straight past his intended victim, jabbing into the muddy path, but Jonas' spear impaled the rider third from the front through his mail-protected back. Surprisingly, despite the force of the blow and the severity of the injury, the man stayed on his horse, tipping forward initially as the long ash spear unbalanced him. Righting himself, he rode on towards the river.

They all did.

Gudrum's four remaining men.

None of them wore helmets, and it quickly became apparent that Gudrum wasn't with them, though Tig certainly was. Aleksander could see one of Gudrum's largest warriors kicking him sharply. He drew his sword, urging his horse out of the tree cover. 'Kill them!' he yelled to his friends, knowing that with one man dead and one well on his way, they could wrap things up quickly and find Gudrum.

Aleksander kicked his boots into his horse's flanks, feeling the first drops of rain. 'Ha! Ha!' He turned at another sound behind him, and suddenly more men were there.

At least another fifteen.

Aleksander felt his heart thump in his chest as their hopes of success shattered.

***

The breeze was freshening again as Eadmund led Eydis away from the warm hall out into the cool afternoon. It was getting darker earlier, he thought to himself, noticing for the first time in weeks how quickly another year was coming to a close.

Another year lost.

Another year alone.

But smiling encouragingly at his sister, he tried not to give in to his gloomy feelings. He thought of Orla Berras and felt odd. 'So tell me, and tell me quickly before Father comes looking for us. He won't be happy I've dragged you out in the cold. You know how he gets.'

Eydis felt warm enough but just as eager to avoid their father as Eadmund. 'You can't marry Orla Berras,' she whispered when they were a few paces from the hall. Eydis could hear muffled voices, the whistle of the wind. Chickens were clucking nearby, the groan of a wagon being pulled through the mud. 'You can't.'

Eadmund's breath caught in his throat. 'Why?'

Eydis stumbled now, not sure what she should say. She had woken from her dream with such a strong feeling, though now everything had started to blur, the dream slipping back into the darkness of her mind. 'I just know that she's not the woman you're supposed to marry.'

Eadmund laughed. 'You must be the only one on the island who thinks so! Everyone else is busy trying to push me into her arms.' He stopped himself, thinking of Evaine. 'Well, not everyone.' He felt cold, and thirsty, impatient with his sister, and then cross with himself for being impatient with his sister. He didn't see much of her these days. She was growing so quickly; no longer a little girl. 'Who am I supposed to marry, then?' he wondered, trying to keep his voice light. Eydis saw with her ears, he knew, and he wanted her to hear that he wasn't bothered.

But something about Orla Berras was troubling him too. Though, after all these years, he doubted anything he thought.

Eydis sighed, frustrated. 'I don't know.' The feeling she had was strange. Her dreams were not even shapes sometimes, just emotions. She knew she had seen something, someone, but she didn't know who or what it was. 'I just know that it's not Orla Berras.'

'Well, that's not especially helpful, Little Thing,' Eadmund said gently, seeing how flustered she was becoming. He grabbed her elbow, trying to stop her swaying about in the wind. 'I know you want to help, but I can't imagine Father will be convinced by just a feeling.' He felt bile rush into his mouth, and he swallowed, looking back to the hall doors. 'Though if you dreamed of an actual reason? Had a real vision?'

Eydis frowned, wanting to think that she had. 'I... I... nothing clear enough yet. Not yet. You just need to trust me, Eadmund. Please, don't marry her.'

Eadmund heard the urgency in Eydis' voice, and he wrapped an arm around her shoulder. 'I do trust you, but I'm not the one you have to convince. Still, if you can find a way to get me out of this marriage, I'll owe you a debt for life!'

Eydis could feel her brother's anxiety rising. She knew that he wanted to break free from his prison, but no matter how much he tried, he was still trapped in there. And time was running out, as both she and Eirik knew too well.

Time was running out for Eadmund to turn things around.

***

Aleksander slammed the pommel of his sword into the chin of a black-bearded warrior riding a dirty white horse.

Not Gudrum. There was still no sign of Gudrum.

The man spat blood at him as he tried to regain his balance, one hand on the cantle. Aleksander reversed his sword, stabbing the tip of his blade into the exposed notch of black-beard's throat. The man's eyes bulged, dark pupils exploding, and he toppled off his horse with a scream, boot still stuck in a stirrup. His horse charged up the riverbank, his fallen rider banging uselessly against the muddy ground like a cloth doll.

Aleksander heard Jonas shout, struggling to keep in his own saddle as he fought off two of Gudrum's men. Isaak was further behind, spinning his horse around, hacking his axe into a man's shoulder, yanking it out, going back for more. Aleksander kept a firm hold of his sword as his horse slipped, jerking around as another of Gudrum's men galloped towards him, winking blade suddenly disappearing in a furious downpour, lightning crackling through the sky.

Aleksander spun again, sensing two more men approaching from his other side. Rain was quickly in his eyes, blurring his vision, running down his face. He shook his head, trying to see, ducking a blade scything towards him. Turning his horse, again and again, he could feel his grip loosen on his sword, his horse slipping in the mud.

Then he was stabbing.

One strike through the cheek of a one-eyed warrior. Deep. Aleksander pushed it in hard, not wanting further problems from that man, spinning around suddenly as the tip of a blade scraped down his arm guard. Pushing himself up, boots pressing down on the stirrups, he stabbed again, through the neck of a bellowing warrior, who gurgled, unable to bellow anymore, his sword dropping uselessly to the ground, hands reaching for his ruined throat.

Aleksander shook dripping hair out of his eyes, trying to see. He heard Jonas crying out in pain. Or was it Isaak? The rain was louder than the clashing of weapons, and now thunder was booming above them, frightening the horses who quickly became even more skittish. He couldn't hear a thing, but he could see that they had to leave. There were too many of Gudrum's men swelling around them now.

They had to cross the river.

CHAPTER NINE

Evaine stood in the garden.

The sky was darkening, and despite the freezing gale pulling at her hair and whipping her dress around her legs, there was no sign of a storm coming. She hated the miserable, bleak island, but the thought of all those cold nights ahead in Eadmund's bed had her smiling.

Ignoring a scowl from a toothless old woman with a basket full of herbs, she quickly focused her attention on the list she had scribbled onto a scrap of vellum. It flapped in her hand as she ducked her head and scurried down a row of angelica, shivering.

There wasn't much time.

She had to hurry.

***

Aleksander swung around, teeth bared, blinking, flicking mud out of his eyes. His horse had slipped on the muddy bank, soaked by the rain and the rising river, and they'd both fallen down with a crash. 'We've got to cross the river!' he yelled to Isaak, trying to get his bearings. Aleksander's horse had run away from him, up the riverbank, loose reins flying as the rain pounded down, drowning out his voice. 'Isaak! Cross the river!'

Despite the thunderous downpour, Gudrum's men could hear him. They sheathed their swords, gathering reins into wet hands as Jonas and Isaak spun their horses around, charging up the bank, mud flying everywhere.

Aleksander didn't follow them.

He turned in the opposite direction, into the rain.

He had to get Tig.

***

Jael walked into the hall alone.

She felt the absence of Aleksander as nearly every pair of eyes turned towards her. The fires were bright and warm, and after the cooling afternoon air, she was grateful for them.

Just not the company.

Lothar eyed her from the high table where his fingers were already slick with grease from the plate of goose and dumplings he was gobbling up. He pointed to one of the tables in front of him. 'I've saved you a seat!' he called, brandishing a leg bone. 'Right where I can keep an eye on you!'

Osbert grinned from his right, eyes glowing in the flames.

Jael ignored him and smiled at his sister Amma, who blinked back at her cousin with a look of embarrassment and sympathy. Jael didn't want sympathy, though. She wanted to know that Aleksander and Tig were alright, and she wanted to be back in her wreck of a cottage, biting her nails, waiting for their return.

There was only one place at the table Lothar was motioning her towards.

Right beside Gant.

Inhaling a sharp breath, Jael squeezed in beside him, keeping her arms and legs well away from his. The strong smell of bacon made her stomach churn, and she looked away as one of Lothar's servants hurried a full plate to her.

She didn't want it.

Oleg sat opposite Jael. Gant beside her.

Both men complicit in helping Lothar claim the throne.

Jael lifted her eyes, trying to avoid theirs, watching her brother, Axl, talking with his friends in the darkest corner of the hall. He barely spoke to her these days, no doubt hoping to avoid another lecture about keeping out of trouble. But frowning at the company he was keeping, Jael knew that sooner or later he was definitely going to get himself in trouble.

'Where's Aleksander?' Oleg wondered quietly.

Jael felt reluctant to even speak. 'Hunting.' Her eyes moved to the ale jug before her, ignoring her plate. She could hear Lothar laughing with Osbert who snorted back at him, their eyes on her.

Gant stiffened. '*Hunting*?'

Jael ignored him, overcome with the sudden urge to leave.

Something was wrong.

It was hard to swallow, the heat from the fires suddenly becoming oppressive.

Her heart started racing.

Something was wrong with Aleksander.

***

The man riding Tig was surprised when Aleksander jumped up at him, grabbing his arm.

'Tig! Up! Up! Come on, boy! Up!'

Tig had been hearing that voice every day for most of his life. And though he was generally a badly behaved horse who hated being told what to do, he had a keen understanding of battle and war.

And he could sense danger all around him.

So when Aleksander yanked on Gudrum's man's arm, trying

to pull him out of the saddle, Tig reared up on his hind legs, helping him on his way.

***

Evaine was panicking as the last glimpses of light were gobbled up by dark clouds.

She peered at the vellum, then down at the rows of herbs at her feet. She had picked out the salvia, sage, and henbane, but she had no idea what the rest of the herbs she needed even looked like.

Soon it would be completely dark.

And then she saw a man.

Evaine tucked her flapping cloak around her shivering body, heading towards him with a smile. 'Entorp!'

Entorp froze in surprise, never having heard Evaine address him with such enthusiasm in all the years he'd lived on Oss. He had his knife out, preparing to add some yarrow to his full basket. His tooth had been aching for days, and though he found himself always busy, caring for others, he needed to do something before it developed into a problem. Turning, Entorp watched as Evaine came rushing towards him, cheeks flushed, eyes alert.

'I need some help!'

'With the plants?' Entorp looked confused.

Evaine nodded. 'My mother sent me to gather some for her, but I don't recognise them all. Or perhaps I wasn't listening carefully enough?' The troublesome wind screeched through the tiny garden, whipping her cloak up into her face. Evaine grabbed hold of it, irritated, struggling to maintain her smile.

'I can help you, of course,' Entorp said. 'What did your mother need?' He liked Runa, and sympathised with her having such a difficult daughter. Perhaps it was youth, he thought more generously, trying not to be too much of an old curmudgeon.

Evaine looked relieved, quickly peering down at the scrunched up piece of vellum again. 'Marshmallow and moonflower.'

Entorp froze. 'Moonflower? What does she need that for? Are you sure you have that right?' He peered at Evaine's basket, trying to see what else she had collected.

'I do.' Evaine quickly pulled the basket towards her. 'I don't know what she does with herbs at all, I'm afraid. I just do what I can to help her.' She stared at Entorp, blinking eyes so full of innocence.

Eventually, Entorp nodded, the pain in his tooth suddenly so demanding that all he could think about was getting back to his warm house and his agreeable cats. 'Alright then, come with me.'

***

Eadmund wasn't the sort of man Orla had dreamed of marrying when she closed her eyes at night. He did not look like a brave warrior or a man destined to become a noble king. He appeared unwell, lost, in need of help. But there was nothing Orla Berras liked more than helping lost creatures. And although she had never tried to help someone in such a bad way before, she felt sure it could be done.

So, as her mother fretted and her father tried to come to terms with finally letting her go, she found herself imagining a life on Oss. A new life as a wife, a mother, and one day, maybe, a queen, free from her fussing parents and the fear of growing into a lonely old spinster. Or equally, the fear of being pushed into marriage with a man she could never love.

Orla smiled, realising that Eadmund Skalleson was most definitely a man she could love in time.

'You are certain, then? Truly?' her mother asked for the eleventh time as she sat on the bed, slipping off a pair of delicate shoes that were completely unsuited to a muddy bog like Oss' square.

'I am,' Orla insisted, spinning around. 'I think there's something there. Something I can work with.'

Cotilde laughed. 'He's not a three-legged dog, Orla! You're not going to fix that man easily.'

'Perhaps,' Orla mused, combing her long hair as she sat by the fire in the centre of their chamber. She had been desperate to untangle her hair and change her dress before returning to the hall, where she would no doubt be expected to sit for yet another meal. 'But there is plenty of time before he becomes the king, isn't there? Eirik Skalleson looks in fine health to me. I'm sure there'll be time to turn everything around.'

Cotilde rolled her eyes as she reached for a clean pair of shoes, remembering all the birds her daughter had retrieved from cats' mouths, believing she could save them. And sometimes she had.

But a man as obviously broken as Eadmund Skalleson?

Cotilde didn't know if such a thing was possible.

***

Aleksander could hear Gudrum's men shouting behind him as he drove Tig into the river, feeling the bracing cold water flood his boots, soaking his trousers. Tig was quiet as he fought through the current that eddied and slapped around his legs, quickly rising to his chest. Lifting his head higher, he could hear Aleksander's familiar deep voice in his ears, keeping him calm.

'Go! This way!'

Aleksander saw glimpses of his friends who were further upstream; Isaak urging Jonas to follow him to where the current appeared more manageable. Neither of their horses were as big as Tig, though, and Aleksander could see that soon they were going to struggle.

The current was stronger than any of them had expected, rain hammering them painfully now, the sky as dirty as the river; grim, grey, and brown, swirling with storm clouds. It was hard to see where the opposite riverbank was.

Aleksander could see a handful of Gudrum's men, though, urging their horses into the water after them. Most remained, lining the sloppy bank, nocking arrows into longbows.

'Get down!' Aleksander yelled in warning, flattening himself against Tig's neck as the first wave of arrows whistled through the deluge. Most dove helplessly into the river, but one hit Isaak's horse on its rump. 'Isaak!'

Isaak wasn't waiting around for more arrows. He kicked his wet boots into his horse's grey flanks, urging her on, and despite the arrow wound leaking blood into the water, she surged forward, fighting the powerful current.

Aleksander could hear Gudrum's men screaming at them.

But Gudrum still wasn't there.

He wiped his wet hair out of his wet eyes, trying to concentrate.

Another wave of arrows.

Aleksander felt Tig tense, roaring in pain.

And then, so was he.

***

Evaine's chest rose and fell in such a panic that she worried she was going to make a mistake. She tried to steady her hand by taking a few deep breaths, but her eyes kept darting to the door, which she had locked, hoping her mother would remain in the hall for some time yet.

Morac was always in the hall, by Eirik's side, the extra pair of eyes his king needed, but Runa had little appetite for the noise and the drinking, and Evaine worried that she would not stay long enough for her to finish. She almost wished she hadn't sent their servant away; the extra pair of hands would have come in handy.

After one more skittery breath, Evaine leaned forward, picking up a handful of moonflower leaves, adding them to the bowl. She needed to blend the mixture thoroughly and then find a way to mask the stink of it. Glancing around, she spied a jar of honey on one of the kitchen shelves.

***

Aleksander's ears were ringing as he clung to Tig's bridle with wet hands. He'd fallen off the saddle, into the river as Tig stumbled sideways; one arrow sticking out of his back, another in his rump as the big horse struggled against the current. Aleksander could feel Tig's muscles straining as he fought to keep his hooves on the muddy sludge of the riverbed. The deeper the water got, the harder it was becoming to keep going in one direction.

Aleksander had an arrow in his shoulder, and the pain as the current moved it around, almost snapping it off, was unbearable. But there were so many other things demanding his attention that he forced himself to focus, determined not to pass out.

They were well away from the riverbank where Gudrum's archers stood now. The rest of Gudrum's rain-drenched men had turned their horses around, heading out of the river, but the arrows were still flying. Terrifying whistles pierced the sheeting rain as Aleksander firmed up his grip on the bridle, trying to see his friends. 'Isaak!' he yelled. 'Jonas!' But there was no reply, and in the deluge he couldn't see anything moving on the river at all. It was suddenly all brown: the sky, the water, the blurry mess before his eyes.

And then the twisting current took Tig's legs out from under him.

Aleksander felt the sudden rush as he lost his own balance, trying to keep hold of Tig, not wanting to let go of Jael's beloved horse.

Still wondering what had happened to Gudrum.

***

Jael had barely spoken while she'd been forced to sit in the hall, listening to Lothar snort and fart, encouraging those around him to praise his masterful leadership as he talked of his plans for conquering Hest.

Lothar was mad.

His men were all mad for going along with him.

And Jael was mad at being forced to listen to such a tirade of ill-informed drivel.

Eventually, seeing that her uncle's attention had wandered to a sad-looking servant girl who squirmed as he pawed her, licking his greasy pink lips, Jael slipped out of the hall. Her mind was tumbling with worries for Aleksander and Tig. Frustration too. She wanted to be the one fighting Gudrum to get Tig back. He was her responsibility. Hers to care for.

She should be the one risking her life for him.

Ending Gudrum too.

It was dark, and Jael had already stumbled twice as she walked through the fort, heading for her cottage, though she doubted she could sit still, or even think about falling asleep. The urgent feeling she'd experienced in the hall had stayed with her, and she felt intense waves of nausea, as though she were at sea.

The nights were definitely getting chillier, and Jael tried not to think about how cold her bed would be without Aleksander and his warm body in it, because that just led her straight back down the path of terror, wondering if he would come back.

Gudrum may have slouched around with an air of arrogance. He may have moved slowly, and his body may have softened and slumped over the years. But he had not lost his edge. He would expect trouble.

Wouldn't he?

Jael suddenly realised that Aleksander should have taken more men.

***

Jonas had lost his horse, but he'd found Aleksander, who had swept past him clinging to Tig. They managed to clasp arms before Aleksander drifted away from him. There was no sign of Isaak, though occasionally the two men thought they heard a shout. Or perhaps that was from Gudrum's men changing their minds, deciding to follow them after all?

The storm had retreated as night came to claim them, but there was no moon or stars to see by, just the sound of the rushing water, freezing their weary limbs. It helped to keep Aleksander alert though. As the pain in his shoulder started to bite, and the exhaustion of holding onto Tig as the force of the current threatened to separate them, his mind would wander, and then, shivering, he would wake himself up, clinging on with greater urgency.

Jonas had a broken arrow sticking out of his forearm. The powerful current had snapped off the fletching, but the shaft was doing its job of keeping the wound as sealed as possible. And, with Aleksander's help, he pushed himself over the top of Tig's saddle, keeping one hand on his bridle as he made his way to the horse's other side.

They could both feel Tig weakening. Shaking.

And firming up their hold on either side of the bridle, Aleksander and Jonas let the river take them all downstream, into the darkness.

***

Evaine was always sticking her nose in everywhere, following her father around the hall, chasing after Eadmund. So, though it was a nuisance, it wasn't a surprise to see her pop up in the kitchen, getting in the way.

Very rarely had Eirik's cook ever had to cope with such important guests, and when the king wasn't entertaining Ake Bluefinn, he was rushing into the kitchen to bark orders, unhappy with the speed at which the food was being delivered into the hall. So Yetta was unimpressed with having to shoo Evaine out of her way just when she needed to hurry the soup course to her grumbling king.

'I can help,' Evaine insisted into Yetta's red face. 'My father suggested that I should.'

It made no sense to Yetta, knowing how lazy Evaine was, but she couldn't deny that she needed an extra pair of hands. Two of her staff were ill. She hadn't seen them all day. 'You can take the soup out with Eryth, then,' she grumbled, wiping a hand over her dripping forehead. It may have been bitterly cold outside, but inside the tiny kitchen, the fires were blazing, and Yetta was dreaming of a dip in the sea. 'But carefully! Addi broke my last tureen, so we're having to take each bowl out one at a time.'

Evaine tried not to smile, bobbing her head as she turned towards the table, her back to Yetta as she leaned over the bowls.

CHAPTER TEN

It felt odd to Eadmund that three old men were planning his future. Two he didn't know, and one who was so fed up with him that he was desperately racing towards the marriage agreement before Eadmund ruined everything.

And Eadmund very much wanted to ruin everything.

With all his heart, he wanted to do something to make Hector Berras change his mind; to make his daughter not want to marry him at all. But Orla turned to Eadmund with a smile, her voice soft in his ear, and he felt his body respond, not sure if any of that was true.

'I wouldn't mind going for a walk,' she whispered. 'What do you think? I've never eaten so much in my life. I could do with stretching my legs before I fall asleep.' She tried not to laugh as she inclined her head down the table to where Torstan lay fast asleep, his blonde head nestled amongst the empty ale jugs and greasy plates as the noise of the hall flowed around him.

Eadmund shook his head, eyes on Thorgils who looked on from across the hall with his mouth hung open, as though he was trying to read their lips. 'A walk?' He didn't know if he could walk anywhere. He'd drunk far too much of that Kalmeran wine his father rarely let out of his sight, but Orla sat back and grinned at him, and Eadmund could see her freckles sparkling in the glow of the torchlight.

So he nodded.

***

Jael stood outside the door of her cottage, taking a long breath, trying to calm herself down. She didn't want to worry Biddy. She'd never hear the end of it if Biddy even got a hint that something was wrong. As far as she knew, Aleksander had gone hunting. There was nothing unusual about that. Jael hated hunting, and since Aleksander didn't mind it, she had always been happy to let him go on his own. So there was nothing Biddy needed to be suspicious about at all, as long as Jael didn't give her any reason to.

Closing her eyes, she could feel the hairs on the back of her neck rise, and spinning around, Jael sensed that feeling again, certain now that something was wrong. She shivered, slipping one hand inside her cloak as she reached for the door handle with the other, disturbed by how dark the cottage was as she stepped inside. And as the door swung shut behind her, her right hand was quickly on the pommel of her father's sword.

'If you want your nursemaid to live, you'll leave that sword right where it is,' growled the voice in warning.

Jael stood with her back to the door, listening. The darkness was almost complete, but she didn't need any light to know who was there.

Boots scuffed across the dirt floor, and she could hear a faint whimpering.

Biddy.

Jael kept her sword in its scabbard, hands by her side now, heart hammering in her chest, fears for Aleksander bright like a newly-sharpened blade. If Gudrum was here, what had he done with Aleksander and Tig?

Where were they?

'So you wanted to kill me after all?' Jael said, trying to think. And then a flame in the fire pit burst into life, and she saw a glimpse of a smirking Gudrum hunched over on the opposite side of the cottage, knife pressed across a terrified Biddy's throat.

The cottage was tiny. A shack with two beds. Biddy's at the

back, Jael and Aleksander's on the left side. A small fire pit in the middle. Shelves and an old barrel on the right. Three tree stumps surrounding the stone-ringed fire.

Narrow. Dark.

Not a place to swing a sword, even if she could unsheath it in time.

'*Kill* you?' Gudrum hissed, anger coating his voice with unvarnished malevolence for the first time. '*Kill* you? Ha! I'm going to gut you, you smug bitch. Gut you and bleed you so you can feel yourself die. If only Aleksander was here to watch, but he's been taken care of by my men. And now there's just one problem left for me to attend to before I meet up with my new horse.'

Jael had to keep him talking.

Keep him talking so she could stitch together a plan.

Quickly.

She couldn't think about Aleksander or Tig.

Not now.

She had to find a way to save Biddy.

***

The cold air helped to sober Eadmund up; that and the discomfort of being completely alone with Orla as they headed across the square. He didn't know where he was taking her. It was a wild, moonless night, and any braziers burning around the square had lost their flames long ago.

Eadmund tried to think of something to say as they headed down an alley. He tried not to walk too close to Orla. He didn't want to make her feel awkward, but most of him just felt awkward himself.

It had been too long.

Far too long.

'It's strange, isn't it?' Orla said, slipping her hand through his arm all of a sudden, sensing Eadmund freeze. She smiled, carrying on, edging even closer as the alley narrowed. 'Our fathers are busy planning our marriage, yet we haven't even spoken about it with each other.' Now she felt awkward. 'I... I don't want you to feel forced into something you don't want, Eadmund. That is no path to happiness, is it?'

The alley was dark with flittering shadows, and Orla didn't even know where they were, but she stopped, trying to see Eadmund's eyes. They remained hidden from her, though, as he swayed before her, head down.

'I...' Eadmund swallowed, looking up. Part of him was working hard to convince the rest of him to take the opportunity to escape before it was too late.

The other part...

'I'm not. You don't need to worry, I'm not.'

'I'm not worried,' Orla assured him. 'I just want you to be happy. To think that we could make each other happy. There's no point to it otherwise, is there?'

'Happy?' It didn't feel possible anymore, but Eadmund realised that he would never know if he didn't try to find out. He looked down at her, wishing he could stand still for just one moment. 'It would be nice to be happy,' he admitted. 'I was once.'

'But not now?'

Eadmund could sense Orla's body urging him to move closer, to touch her, to kiss her, but his boots wouldn't budge.

That didn't stop Orla, who leaned forward, placing a hand on his cheek.

'I don't know,' he mumbled, surprised when she pushed herself up onto her toes, her lips seeking his. He lowered his head, closing his eyes. 'I don't know.'

And then Orla stumbled to one side with a gasp.

Eadmund's eyes sprung open, and he grabbed her arm, feeling her go limp. 'Are you alright?'

She shook her head, overcome with nausea, dizzy, ears ringing. 'No, no, I think you'd better take me back to the hall.' She started shaking. 'I need to lie down.'

'Come this way,' Eadmund urged, an arm around Orla's shoulder, turning down another alley. 'It leads around the back of the hall. Much quicker than the way we came. I'll get you back to your chamber through there.'

***

The small flame was going out, and Gudrum and Biddy sank back into the shadows. Jael tried to hold on to everything she had seen, wanting to remember precisely how he was holding Biddy; where his knife was. 'You think killing me will make you feel better? After all these years? You think you'll miss your son any less because I'm ash?'

'*Ash*?' Gudrum was growling again, increasing the pressure of the blade against Biddy's pulsing throat. She yelped, trying to stop herself shaking, desperate to keep perfectly still. 'You think I'll leave enough of you to waste a flame on? It's been a long time since you've seen what I can do with a knife, Jael Furyck.' He spat her name, standing taller now, one arm still around Biddy's throat as he grabbed a lamp from a small table beside her bed.

Jael could smell fish, and she knew the lamp had been burning recently. Biddy struggled to see clearly, and she would have lit that lamp as soon as dusk had signalled its approach.

Gudrum threw the fish oil into the fire pit, and that lone flame sparked brightly, more flames quickly joining in. 'But first, you can watch me rip out this old bitch's eyes.'

Now a fire burned between them, and they could see each other clearly.

'Don't move!' Gudrum ordered, sensing Jael twitch.

Biddy whimpered, trying not to move at all, feeling the sharp edge of the blade lift away from her throat, up, over her face.

'Biddy?'

Jael could hear Edela's voice outside the door, and so could

Gudrum. His eyes darted towards it, and Jael lifted her left hand, flinging it towards his head as he turned back to her.

Biddy shrieked in terror as the tiny throwing knife whipped through the air towards her, over her, landing in Gudrum's raised hand. He roared, jerking his hand away from Biddy's throat, fingers splayed in pain, knife dropping to the dirt floor. Biddy stumbled down to the ground, crawling quickly, desperate to escape Gudrum, who suddenly needed a weapon more than a prisoner. Caught between picking up his knife and drawing his sword, Gudrum scooped up the knife with his left hand, teeth gleaming as Jael lunged around the flames towards him, drawing her own knife from its scabbard.

'Biddy?'

Biddy was on her hands and knees, crawling away from Gudrum towards the door, but he skipped around the fire, out of Jael's path, blocking it.

None of them wanted Edela coming inside.

'Go away, Grandmother!' Jael cried. 'We'll see you in the morning!' She didn't need another target for Gudrum. 'Go away! We're sleeping!'

There was no sound as Gudrum and Jael stalked around the fire, moving from side to side, trying to avoid tripping over the stools, waiting to see who would be the first to pounce. Blood poured from Gudrum's hand, his lips peeled back, the pain of his wound revealing itself. His yellow-tinged eyes glowed with anger, though, as he tried to focus. He had to work quickly before that nosey old dreamer alerted anyone to trouble. 'Got any more baby knives?' he spat, jerking his knife at Jael. 'You want to prick me to death? That's how your fuck of a father taught you to fight? *Baby knives?*'

Jael's temper spiked, and she dipped away from him, leaning her weight onto her left leg, kicking Gudrum with her right. He stumbled towards the fire, quickly righting himself before the flames could do much more than singe his cloak. Jumping back, he avoided Jael's next blow, pushing his boots against the dirt, firming up his grip on his knife, knowing that he'd never been particularly strong with his left hand.

Trying not to let it unsettle him.

'He did. Showed me how to hurt people with them. Big knives too.' And Jael flicked her right wrist, flinging her knife at Gudrum's throat.

He dropped his head as the blade whipped through the smoke, just past his ear, falling to the ground.

Jael's breath was pumping fast as she stumbled after him, drawing another knife from her swordbelt. She wasn't cold now. The heat from the fire beckoned as they danced around it, one knife each; flames threatening the tips of fingers, licking the hems of their flapping cloaks.

'And when you lose that knife, little girl?' Gudrum taunted, cocky smile firmly back in place now, ignoring the pain in his hand. 'What will you do to me then?'

'Well, there's always my teeth,' Jael panted. 'I've still got all of them.' And she swapped her remaining knife into her right hand, trying to remember if Gudrum was strong with his left, but it was too many years since they'd last fought, and she couldn't.

Biddy watched them both, crouching by her bed, trying to think. She needed to help Jael. And she couldn't do that if she got herself captured by that revolting man again.

The fire was blazing in the cottage now, and her eyes drifted back to the door, hoping she could find a way to escape and get some help.

***

Aleksander grabbed the hand Isaak held out. He shook so much that he wasn't sure he could even drag himself out of the river, but getting out of the water was imperative now. They all had to find a way to get warm quickly. Tig too.

Isaak jumped down into the freezing river, grabbing hold

of Tig's bridle as Aleksander and Jonas crawled up the bank, collapsing onto the slippery mud.

Isaak was the strongest of the three, not having an arrow leaking blood like the other two, and he dragged a weak Tig up after them, past the mud and onto the grass where Tig shook himself, flinging cold water all over them.

Then promptly fell to the ground.

'Tig! Shit!' Aleksander was up on his feet, slipping and sliding his way in the dark, trying to find the horse who was now just a big lump hidden in the shadows.

Isaak's horse had made it across the river with him, and she stood nearby, shaking in front of a tree.

'We need a f-fire!' Aleksander called, teeth chattering as he squatted down next to Tig. 'We need to see!'

Jonas fell onto his back, panting. 'We need to see to find anything to light a fire with in the first place!'

'I'll go,' Isaak sighed, too cold to argue. 'Hopefully, Gudrum's men aren't looking for us.'

'Doubt they followed us in that storm,' Aleksander muttered, feeling around Tig's frozen rump, finding a broken arrow sticking out of it. 'Not down the river, at least.'

Isaak didn't answer. He'd already disappeared into the trees, looking for anything that wasn't wet, which was unlikely after such a furious downpour.

Jonas sat up, shaking his long wet hair. 'How is he?' he wondered, thinking about his own horse, lost in the river. He'd appeared to be a good swimmer, though, so there was still a chance of finding him. 'Tig? How is he?'

Aleksander placed his hand on Tig's head. 'I don't know,' he admitted, worry gripping him like an iron hand. He thought of Gudrum, hoping he hadn't gone after Jael.

Fearing the answer.

'I don't know.'

***

Jael had lost her last knife, though Gudrum had a gaping wound to show for it, part of his cheek flapping open, blood sheeting down his hairy face, soaking his beard.

She tore off her cloak, the silver brooch ripping through the woven cloth as she threw it at her bed, hoping that Biddy would stay crouching where she was.

She didn't need to worry about her now.

Jael's eyes remained on Gudrum who still had his cloak on, mail shirt gleaming beneath it. He kept jerking from side to side in the cramped space between the fire and her bed, not giving her an easy target to aim for; smart enough to sense what she was trying to do.

But now Jael had no cloak. Nothing in her hands at all.

And she leaped over the flames towards Gudrum, aiming low.

Gudrum's mouth fell open in surprise, dropping his knife as Jael knocked him back onto the bed. He reacted quickly, though, using his weight to flip her over. He was a powerful man, arms like rocks, pressing his weight down on Jael as she tried to wriggle away from him, up the bed. Gudrum punched her cheek, smacking her head back onto the pillow. He pulled back his fist, ready to hit her again, but Jael jerked away, releasing a hand to jab him in the throat.

'You bitch!' Gudrum rasped, spitting in Jael's face as she punched him in the eye. He slapped her, knocking her back onto the pillow again, leaning all his weight down on one arm as he scooped up his knife from the floor, blinking, trying to see.

'No!' Biddy shrieked as Gudrum brought the blade up to Jael's throat.

Jael tried to move, but Gudrum was leaning more and more of his weight on her, and she was struggling to lift an arm or a leg. The bed was creaking and groaning as she thrashed about, desperate to pull her head away from that knife.

Gudrum grinned, sensing her panic as she fought to move him.

'Good with a sword, good with a knife, but how about wrestling, Furia's daughter? With the weight of a real man on top of you?' He pushed himself down onto her, shunting his body against hers, grunting. 'How good are you at that?'

Jael roared, slamming her head forward, aiming for Gudrum's bleeding cheek. He ducked to the side, laughing, enjoying the feel of her squirming beneath him. His body throbbed with both pleasure and pain as he lifted the tip of his blade to Jael's chin. 'Hold steady now, princess, or you'll end up dead before we've had any fun.'

'Grrrr!' Biddy threw herself at Gudrum's back, trying to grab a handful of his cloak, hoping to pull him off Jael before he could hurt her.

Irritated, Gudrum swung a fist at Biddy, knocking her into the flames.

'Biddy!' Jael screamed, quickly reaching under the pillow, and as Gudrum turned his attention back to her, she stabbed the knife she'd retrieved into his shoulder, pushing it straight through his cloak, through the iron links in his mail. She could feel his body jerk, lifting up, his back arching in pain. And pushing him off her, Jael fell off the bed, crawling to Biddy, dragging her out of the fire.

Flames were licking Biddy's apron; her hair was smoking.

'Jael? Jael!' Edela was outside the door again.

With warriors. Voices Jael thought she recognised.

Gudrum was roaring and cursing behind her, and Biddy was on fire before her. Jael ignored Gudrum and threw Biddy to the ground, rolling her like a rug, trying to douse the flames, turning back as Gudrum lunged at her again, bloody teeth bared, knife sweeping towards her face.

Then the cottage door swung open with a bang.

'No!' Jael yelled as Gudrum blinked at her, panic in his eyes. 'No! Don't let him go!' But seeing the two warriors Edela had quickly found to help her, Gudrum ran for the door, realising that his hopes of killing Jael Furyck and disappearing without being discovered were diminishing by the moment. Jael tried to grab his cloak as he flew past, knocking the two men into each other, sending them tumbling.

Edela screamed, stumbling away as Gudrum drew his sword, stabbing one man through the chest, swinging around, slashing his bloody blade across the throat of the other.

His eyes met Jael's before he turned and ran.

Jael glanced down at Biddy who was no longer on fire.

'Go!' Biddy panted, pain contorting her face. 'Go!'

And Jael scrambled to her feet, eyes on her grandmother who didn't know which of Gudrum's victims to help first. 'Stay with Biddy!' she cried, running out of the cottage into the pitch-black night, seeing the flap of Gudrum's cloak ahead of her, sensing that he was running for the main gates.

She was faster than that old man, she was sure. And with both gates locked at sundown every night, he would have no way out.

***

Eadmund fell down onto his creaking bed.

It was cold, he realised, momentarily lost.

Wasn't it supposed to be summer?

Thoughts of summer and warmth led him to thoughts of Orla, and flopping back onto the pillow, his mind whirled with confusion. Orla had not looked well when he'd left her chamber, but her servant had been there to assure him that likely the three days of feasting had finally taken their toll.

Orla had smiled weakly as he'd closed the door, apologising, looking forward to seeing him in the morning.

That smile and those kind eyes were a constant reminder that the light was just a step away. If only he could leave the shadows behind...

***

Jael's scabbard slapped against her leg as she ran through the dark fort, chest burning with effort, scattering a pair of brawling cats, their high-pitched wails shattering the silence. Braziers glowed around the edges of the empty square, flames buffeted by a strengthening breeze.

She saw glimpses of Gudrum and the main gates looming in front of him like an enormous shield wall. He was struggling, and Jael dug in deeper, knowing that soon he would have to stop.

But, as Gudrum neared the gates, Jael suddenly realised that they weren't locked. And more surprising still, one was slightly ajar.

'No!' she yelled. 'Shut the gates! Shut the fucking gates!' Her mind was too slow, too overwhelmed with thoughts of catching Gudrum to think about what that meant at first. 'Stop him!'

There were no guards by the gates, though, only those up in the towers, walking around the ramparts. None responded to her, and, in the next breath, Jael watched as Gudrum slipped out of the fort.

She slid through the gates after him, still hoping to catch him. In the darkness, though, she was struggling to see where he'd gone, but a horse's whinny focused her attention, and Jael was quickly running towards the sound, seeing glimpses of Gudrum now as he ran ahead of her.

And then she was down, tripping over a rock, twisting her ankle. She was back on her feet quickly, though, limping, rock in hand. It was a big rock, an ankle breaker, and gritting her teeth, Jael threw it at the running shadow with every bit of strength she had.

It took Gudrum in the back, just below his neck, and he grunted, tumbling to the ground. Jael ran for him, unsheathing her sword, needing to stop him reaching his horse.

A grey horse, she noticed. Not Tig.

Gudrum staggered back to his feet, spitting gravel and blood as he spun around, sword quickly in front of him, head pounding.

'You really want to die, don't you, bitch?'

Jael couldn't put her weight down on her left ankle. She couldn't catch her breath, but she hobbled towards Gudrum, around him, wanting to block his path to the horse. 'No, but I am going to kill you.'

The moon finally shook off its cloudy cloak, revealing the blood-stained wreck of a man standing before her. But Jael could sense there was strength in him still, and she knew that she had to put him down quickly. Jerking her sword forward, she tried to unbalance him, but both of Gudrum's ankles worked just fine, and he merely shifted his weight, lashing out with his own sword, unbalancing her. Jael stumbled, biting her tongue, annoyed, righting herself as she parried his strike, trying to think, but Gudrum quickly attacked her again. There was weight behind his blow, and Jael's arm shuddered as she pushed her right boot back, into the dirt, working hard to hold her ground. Sounds of movement came from the fort, and Jael hoped it was those guards on the wall finally coming to life. 'You tried to take my horse! Tried to kill Aleksander!' she cried, wanting to keep his attention on her.

'Tried to?' Gudrum laughed, and smiling, he lunged, sweeping his sword towards Jael's chest. She jumped back, landing on her left ankle, yelping as she dragged her blade across his thigh, hearing it scrape mail.

Gudrum pushed his boots down, two hands on his sword now, swinging for Jael's head. He knew he didn't have long before his injuries took a toll; his ears were ringing, blood leaking steadily from his cheek, his shoulder, his hand.

He had to end her quickly.

Jael ducked the scything blade, watching Gudrum's cloak billow away from him, revealing just how long his mail shirt was.

He was quickly at her again, focusing her attention, lunging forward with his arm extended, blade reaching for her chest. Jael dipped to the right, leaning all her weight onto her good ankle, switching her sword to her left hand, hacking her blade into Gudrum's with such force that she saw fear flash in his eyes; the fear that he was about to drop his sword. His hand was bloody, she could see, fingers dripping, but they closed around his grip tightly as he jabbed again, trying to get through her guard.

Jael back-handed his blade away, jerking her body from side to side, wanting to tire him out, blocking his next strike which clanged against her blade, unbalancing her again.

And this time, Jael dropped her own sword.

Gudrum's surprise froze him for a moment, before he smiled, launching a powerful blow at Jael's throat.

But Jael skidded to the ground, onto her knees, swaying back, hair brushing the dirt, sliding under Gudrum's sword as it arced towards her face. And scooping her sword into her right hand, she straightened up, dragging the blade across his unprotected knees. Falling to the side, she rolled quickly, hopping back onto her feet, knowing that she'd cut him deep, right to the bone.

Crouching. Waiting.

Wondering what he'd do next.

Gudrum staggered before Jael, mouth wrenched open, eyes fixed on her, sword lingering in mid-air for a moment before dipping as he collapsed to his bleeding knees, falling onto his side, roaring with pain.

Jael brought her sword into both hands, eyes on his neck, taking a quick breath, ready to end him. And as Gudrum turned his head up to look at her, bloody teeth bright in the moonlight, he started to smile.

Jael frowned, confused. But in the next breath, she wasn't.

'Best you put that sword away... my lady.'

Jael spun around, eyes on the four guards who were quickly surrounding her, weapons drawn.

Lothar's men.

And Gudrum, laughing and seething and bleeding Gudrum, was quickly back on his feet, hobbling between two of the guards who had helped him to stand, and were now hurrying him towards his horse, unsteady, leaking blood, but very much alive.

'What are you doing?' Jael shouted, her voice shattering the silence, trying to see anything in the eyes of the two guards who remained, swords pointing at her, but shadows masked their faces.

'What are you *doing*?'

And then the glinting tip of a blade jerked towards her chest. 'Sheath your sword now. *Do it!*'

Or what?

Jael vibrated with rage, wanting to scream it out loud, but there was no point.

Her body heaved, shoulders dropping as the full weight of reality sunk in.

There was no point at all.

She turned her head, watching as Lothar's men boosted a weak Gudrum up onto his horse. There was nothing cocky about him now as the pain took hold. He fell over the saddle, groaning, gathering the reins into bloody hands, sword sheathed, weakly tapping his boots against his horse's flanks, desperate to be gone.

Jael turned back around, wanting to see the eyes of the men who had stopped her. Wanting to remember them. Trying not to think about Gudrum.

And finally, sheathing her father's sword, she lifted her head and limped towards the gates, listening to the whinny of a horse, and the pounding of urgent hooves disappearing into the distance.

CHAPTER ELEVEN

Eadmund felt terrible when he woke up, forced awake by his angry father, who was roughly shoving his shoulder. 'What? What?' His tongue tangled in his dry mouth, and he coughed, trying to swallow, trying to see his father. It was morning, he thought, though the light in the cottage was grim and dull.

It could have been any time of day.

'What did you *do*?' Eirik growled. 'They're leaving!'

Eadmund shook his head. 'What? Who?' He blinked open his eyes, struggling to sit up. 'What do you mean?'

'Orla! Her family. Ake too. All of them! Leaving! The sun's barely up, and they're leaving!'

'I...' Eadmund didn't know why his father was so angry at him. He had no memory of the night before at all as he sat up, gripping his head. 'I didn't do anything. I...' He wasn't sure that was true. He couldn't remember a thing.

Thorgils stomped into the cottage, red-nosed and frowning. 'She's not hanging around out there,' he muttered, eyeing Eadmund. 'She's already on the beach!'

'*What*?' Eirik felt sick. All he had worked so hard to achieve, undone in one night. All of it! All because of Eadmund.

He was livid. Mad with himself for being such a fool.

'You will get out of this fucking bed and come and apologise!' Eirik yelled. '*Now!*'

Eadmund was instantly just as angry. He wasn't a boy, and he felt certain that whatever had happened, he hadn't done anything wrong. 'To who? For what?' He glared at his father, who stood at the end of his bed, then up at Thorgils who towered over him with a pair of disappointed eyes. 'What did I do?'

'No idea! Ask Orla. Her father has torn up the marriage agreement. They want to leave. Sounds like they *are* leaving! And all because of you!' Eirik shook his head. 'Of course it's because of you!'

Eadmund stood, which was a mistake, and he quickly sat back down again, his head spinning. 'I didn't do anything,' he insisted weakly. 'Nothing.' Dropping his head to his hands, he desperately tried to find any memories of the night before. He saw Orla's smiling face, her hand on his arm, her lips lifting towards his.

And then what?

What could he have done?

Thorgils threw Eadmund's cloak at him, and Eirik dragged him to his feet. 'I've reached the end of my patience with you, Eadmund, I truly have!' He turned for the door, desperate to get down to the beach and see what was happening. 'Now, hurry up before I do something I'll likely regret!'

Eadmund frowned after his father, blinking at Thorgils who kept glaring at him. 'I didn't do anything,' he croaked, but Thorgils spun around and headed out of the cottage after Eirik.

***

Orla was hysterical as she stumbled across the beach with her mother, Hector hurrying behind them, hoping that Cotilde could get some sense out of their daughter. She had woken up crying before dawn in a terrible state: sweat soaking her nightdress, hair stuck to her face, wild-eyed. He'd never seen her like that before. She kept muttering about wanting to leave; not wanting to marry Eadmund Skalleson; needing to get away from him.

And then the screaming had started.

Ake was not especially sympathetic as he waited on the black stones, tired eyes darting back and forth from the Berras' to his helmsmen who were hastily preparing his two ships for their unexpectedly early departure. He saw Eirik coming down the hill, a dishevelled looking Eadmund trying to keep up with him, Thorgils bringing up the rear. Ake sighed, blaming himself. Orla was a sweet girl; a woman, he chided himself. Smart and kind. The idea of a marriage had made sense, and he'd thought that it would work out, in spite of Eadmund's problems.

He should have known it would all end in tears.

'Eirik!' he called, hand in the air as he walked towards him.

Eirik approached quickly, slipping on the stones, searching Ake's face for some sign as to which way the wind was blowing. And seeing the Alekkan king's sleepy grin, he carried on, trying to control both his beard and his cloak. Waves surged in the distance, smashing against the shore, and he felt pains in his chest, his body shaking with anger. But what should he have expected, Eirik wondered crossly. This is who Eadmund had become.

Why should he have expected anything else?

'I didn't do anything,' Eadmund insisted into the wind as Thorgils walked along beside him, though his pleas sounded pathetic and empty to his own ears; he still couldn't remember what had happened.

Thorgils could tell. Eadmund's voice was reed-thin.

'Get him away from me!' Orla yelled in the distance, seeing Eadmund approach, orange hair whipping around her pale face. 'Get him away! Hurry! Hurry! We have to leave! *Please!*'

Eadmund's eyes bulged in surprise, listening to the terror in her voice.

Eirik spun around irritably. 'Take him back up the hill!' he growled, eyes on Thorgils. '*Now!*'

Thorgils was surprised by the venom in his king's voice, and he blinked as Eirik spun away, hurrying to where Ake had stopped, waiting for him. 'Come on,' Thorgils said, seeing for the first time the genuine confusion in Eadmund's eyes. It dampened his anger, quickly replacing it with pity. Eadmund didn't even appear to know what was happening. 'Let's get you back up to the fort. Maybe have something to eat? I could do with a hot meal, that's for sure.'

'But...' Eadmund dug his boots into the stones. The wind was fierce, and he shivered into it, his hair blowing away from his face, waking him up. Visions flashed in front of his eyes: Orla smiling, laughing, her arm through his, shyly talking about the future. 'I need to talk to her. I don't know what happened.'

'Best you leave it,' Thorgils warned, his shoulders sinking as he turned away from the screeching wind. 'You'll only make it worse. Whatever you did, she didn't like it, my friend.' He didn't know what to think as he put an arm around Eadmund's back, urging him towards the hill. 'Let's go get a table at Ketil's. Something to eat might stir up some memories.'

Eadmund hung his head, trying to focus on putting one foot after the other, eyes on the stones. He didn't know what to think. Part of him felt relieved, he supposed, knowing that he'd escaped the threat of marriage. Part of him was dulled to everything that was happening around him, as though he wasn't really there at all.

But most of him was just confused, wondering what he had done to Orla.

Evaine stood on the hill with Morac, watching Thorgils help Eadmund across the beach.

'We should go,' Morac grumbled, though he wasn't unhappy. A strong alliance with Ake would have benefitted the islands, and Oss especially, but he had become worried that Eirik and Ake had far too much in common. They had quickly become as thick as thieves, and Morac didn't want anyone to have more sway over Eirik than he did.

That would not do at all.

It was better if they were not brought even closer together with a marriage.

And now, there was no chance of that happening.

'But I want to help Eadmund,' Evaine insisted.

'I think you've helped him enough already,' Morac said.

'Don't you? Best you slip away now. Let the dust settle. Eirik will be screaming the fort down soon, threatening to banish Eadmund to the ends of the earth again. It will take some time to calm him down.'

Evaine looked anxious. 'You won't let that happen, will you? Father? You won't let him send Eadmund away from me?'

Morac smiled. 'Of course not. I won't. But for now, you should go. Stay out of trouble. And stay out of Eirik's way. He doesn't like you anywhere near Eadmund, you know that.'

The thought of Eirik Skalleson trying to get in between her and Eadmund made Evaine's body throb with rage, but she nodded at her father. She trusted him to protect her from Eirik. To keep Eadmund safe. And lifting the hood of her white cloak over her head, Evaine quickly disappeared through the gates as Eadmund and Thorgils struggled up the hill towards the fort.

***

Jael and Biddy were on their way to Edela's cottage. Jael was worried about Aleksander and Tig. Biddy wanted Edela's help convincing Jael to let her stitch her top lip which continued to bleed on and off, and she wanted a salve to help with some of the bruising and swelling on Jael's face; not to mention her ankle, which was a swollen mess that had her limping along.

Though Biddy hadn't told Jael that.

They ran into Lothar and Osbert as they passed the hall.

Lothar stumbled back in surprise, the sun in his eyes, the sight of his niece rendering him mute.

Osbert, though not surprised to see Jael, was shocked by the mess of her face. 'What happened?'

Jael ignored Osbert, her eyes on Lothar who looked as though he'd swallowed his tongue. 'Uncle, you seem lost for words. You weren't expecting to see me this morning?' She held her ground, though she could feel Biddy grip her arm tightly, trying to pull her away.

Lothar squinted, eyes sweeping across Jael's face before becoming suddenly very interested in the clamour down on the piers as two ships made their way into the harbour. 'I was not expecting to see you in such a state, that is certain,' he huffed. 'It's a shame you do not take after your mother. What an elegant lady she is. No wonder you've never found yourself a husband. I'm sure your father gave up trying. Hard to sell a sow when people are looking to buy a prize mare.'

Biddy felt her own temper spark, but having lived with Jael for twenty-seven-years now, she had gotten very good at holding her tongue, and she dropped her eyes, saying nothing.

'I was attacked in my cottage last night. As was Biddy. By Gudrum Killi.'

Osbert's face showed surprise and shock.

Lothar's eyes were evasive, still trying to look past Jael towards the harbour. He acted as though he wasn't even listening. 'Is that so? Seems an odd thing to happen.'

'Odd?' Osbert was more curious. 'How did he get in? Where did he go?'

Those were good questions, Jael thought, staring at her uncle whose dark moustache was twitching, one leg shaking beneath his cloak. 'I've no idea, though I'd be interested to know.' She turned to Osbert. 'He tried to kill me, after all. Not in a fair fight. He wasn't brave enough for one of those. I suppose he didn't think he was good enough.'

'And what did you do to him?' Osbert wondered, eyes on his father now.

'Enough that it would hurt. Not enough that it would kill him. You've no need to worry, Uncle,' Jael said. 'I'm sure we'll be seeing Gudrum Killi again one day.' And motioning for Biddy to walk on, she frowned at Lothar, ignored Osbert, and limped off towards Edela's cottage.

Osbert swung around to his father as Jael strode away. 'You let Gudrum in? To kill Jael?'

Lothar lifted his nose in the air, eyes on the piers. 'Smells like spices. Men with skins and furs too. Why don't we take a look?' And he shuffled away before Osbert could ask him anything else, hoping that Gudrum would head for Alekka now and stay far away from Osterland.

***

Tig was on his feet, but he was weak and so were they, so Aleksander, Jonas, and Isaak walked him and Isaak's horse to the village of Norbo, which was only a morning's journey from the riverbank they had crawled out onto. The sun was out, no sign of rain on the horizon, though the three men and two horses still felt frozen solid as they ambled down the muddy track.

Aleksander didn't want to walk at all. He wanted to run straight back to Andala. Gudrum had tricked them. And they hadn't been clever enough to see it coming.

He wanted to scream.

He kept telling himself that Jael could handle Gudrum Killi.

But if she hadn't seen him coming?

Aleksander was so lost in his thoughts that he didn't hear Isaak talking to him.

'Think we need to slow down. Tig looks ready to drop.'

Aleksander blinked, turning to Jael's horse with concern. 'You alright, boy?' he murmured, running a hand down Tig's black muzzle, worried by how quiet and still he continued to be. Tig was usually twitching, impatient, determined to go somewhere. Just like Jael. But his head drooped, and he barely lifted an eyelid as Aleksander leaned in close, whispering in his ear. 'Why don't we stop for a while? Take a rest?' He turned to Isaak. 'You go on. Both of you. I'll catch up. See if you can find a healer in Norbo.' Aleksander stopped, trying to catch his breath. His ears had been buzzing on and off, and he kept seeing dark patches flash across his eyes. Blood had been steadily leaking from his shoulder all morning.

They all needed a healer; someone to stitch them up.

Isaak's weary eyes were scanning the road, checking the bushes. 'If you're not there by midday, I'll come back.'

'We both will,' Jonas put in with a smile. 'With the healer.'

Aleksander nodded, eyes on an old tree with a broad trunk, thinking how ready he was for a rest too. Just a little rest and they could both get on the road again. He tugged gently on Tig's reins, leading him towards the tree, stumbling slightly, ears ringing louder now.

***

Edela was cross at herself for not seeing Gudrum's plotting earlier. When she'd finally had a vision of what he was up to with Lothar, she'd hurried to find Jael, but by then it had been too late. She'd heard it in Jael's voice, knowing that she was already fighting for her life in that tiny cottage.

Yet Jael had lived, as had Biddy. And though she was grateful for that, guilt lay like a heavy weight on her heart, knowing the poor men she had asked to help her save Jael had both lost their lives.

Edela held her granddaughter's hand which jiggled impatiently in hers while Biddy leaned over Jael, stitching her lip. 'You won't make it go any faster if you wriggle,' she warned, remembering Jael as a girl, the biggest wriggler of all. She would never sit for a cuddle. Ever.

'But what about Aleksander?' Jael asked, ignoring her grandmother. 'What about Tig?'

'Stop talking!' Biddy snapped, trying to concentrate, needle poised near Jael's upper lip. 'I'll stitch you through the nostril in a moment!'

Edela almost grinned, but worry about Aleksander quickly had her frowning as she creaked forward, eyes seeking answers in the twisting flames of her fire. 'Well, Aleksander's surely clever enough to see trouble coming, isn't he? And he can handle himself with a sword, you know that better than anyone.' They were empty words, though, and Edela knew that Jael would not be fooled or comforted by them.

Jael wasn't.

She sat quietly, wondering what she could do.

Lothar had helped Gudrum. She had looked into her uncle's eyes, seen his surprise that she was still standing. And Aleksander was gone. If she disappeared to look for him, what would happen to Gisila, Edela, and Biddy? They were vulnerable without her and Aleksander to look after them. And Axl was no use. She hadn't seen much more than a glimpse of him in days.

Biddy stepped back, squinting at Jael's lip. It was only a couple of stitches, and she doubted there would even be much of a scar. Not like that one running under her eye, which was still angry after all these years. Biddy smiled sadly, thinking how many years it had been since Jael was a girl.

How many since they had felt safe in the fort.

Jael turned to Edela. 'You have to try and dream of Aleksander. Please. And Tig. I need to know what's happened. Where they are. I need to find a way to help them, but I have to know where they are first. If they're alright.'

Edela nodded. 'I will. I barely slept last night, so I may just wrap a fur around myself and fall asleep in front of the fire. Don't worry.' She patted Jael's hand and promptly started yawning. 'Don't worry, now. I'll find them.'

***

Ake Bluefinn was a man of reputation, standing, honour, and most of all, he thought to himself, of family. And he could feel Eirik's fury at his son lifting off him like steam rising from a hot pool of water. He shivered, thinking how nice that sounded on a day this bitter where his toes were curling in his sodden boots, trying to keep each other warm. Where his nose was dripping, and he wished he had more hair on his head or a thick beard like Eirik Skalleson.

He smiled as they walked to his favourite ship, *Camilla*. Named for his mother.

Ake Bluefinn was a man of family.

He turned to Eirik with a grin. 'Our alliance will hold,' he insisted, watching Eirik's small eyes pop open in surprise. 'Whatever your son did to Orla will not break it.' He stopped, watching the Berras', knowing that while Hector might take a while to come around to his position, ultimately, he would have no choice in the matter. 'We're going to need our alliance. My dreamer sees a dark cloud coming. A white cloud too.'

Eirik looked confused, and Ake laughed. 'I've no idea! Sometimes, with that woman, I simply have no idea. She has no teeth. It's a struggle!' His eyes, watering with the cold, were bright and kind. 'But she wanted me to reach out to you. After all these years, it made sense. We're not men who need to build our reputations. Not any longer. We're kings who need to prepare for the future. For our children. Our families.' He turned to the harbour entrance in the distance, watching two ships approach those dangerous stone spires. 'And it's better to know your neighbours as friends, than to continually battle them as enemies.'

Eirik nodded. 'It is.' He felt his stiff shoulders relax slightly for the first time all morning. 'Though I am sorry for whatever offense my son has caused. He is...' Eirik's anger receded quickly, seeing Eadmund's face in his mind. 'He's a good man. An honourable man. I don't understand what he could have done.' He shook his head. 'Though the girl certainly looks upset.'

'That she does,' Ake agreed, watching as Cotilde tried to calm her daughter who was still sobbing, occasionally shrieking. 'Though better to have gone wrong before the marriage than in the middle of it!' He yawned, walking towards the frothing water, eager to be underway, sensing that his helmsmen were ready to put out to sea. If the wind strengthened any further, they would have trouble easing out of the tricky harbour.

Eirik didn't say anything. Some days his love for his son filled him with joy, but mostly he was just brimming with frustration and impatience. He had loved Eadmund's mother fiercely, and his dream had always been to put her son on the throne. He didn't want to think that he would have to abandon him now. That he would be forced into making another choice. One that even he would find it hard to live with. But, Eirik realised, it was time to start thinking about the future of Oss without Eadmund in it.

He had simply run out of time.

***

Eadmund left Thorgils with Torstan who was heading into the hall. He wanted to be alone. His friends barely grunted at him as he left, and he could feel their disappointment following him like a stray dog.

Avoiding everyone's eyes, Eadmund skirted the long tables where a row of red-cheeked women were gutting fish, throwing each part into a different barrel: some to be salted, some dried, and the rest for lamp oil. The overpowering smell had him retching, and the sound of Orla Berras' hysterical screeching taunted him, and Eadmund felt trapped, wanting to grab his horse and ride down the island.

Then he remembered that his horse had died years ago.

He'd never even bothered to find another.

The air was bitter as he trudged along, dense clouds sweeping across the sky, snow flurries settling in his beard, his mouth; his mother's voice in his ears, trying to soothe him, to cheer him up.

Eadmund ignored it, not wanting to feel even more pathetic.

Even more alone.

And then Evaine was there, white cloak bright in a sea of greys and browns, face glowing with happiness to see him. 'Eadmund!' Her blue eyes blinked rapidly as she smoothed down her loose hair, trying to tame the tangles the wind had wrought. She looked up at him with sympathy as he stopped in front of her, reaching out a mittened hand, clasping his. 'Why don't we go back to your cottage?' she smiled eagerly. 'It's so cold out here today. I can help you light a fire. Find some ale to drink.'

Eadmund stared down at her, suddenly aware of how thick the mud was. How cold and wet his feet were in his boots. How much his head ached. How miserable he felt. Memories flickered of his father's rage-filled face. He heard his mother's urgent voice telling him to turn around.

But he found himself nodding, numb, his hand in Evaine's as she led him down the alley, towards his cottage.

CHAPTER TWELVE

Days passed, and Jael was still without Aleksander and Tig.

Edela had seen no sign of Tig in her dreams, though she had seen Aleksander and his two friends, who appeared to be injured, slowly making their way back to Andala. There was some comfort in that. But Edela had not seen her horse, and that worried Jael as she limped around the fort, trying to keep out of Lothar's way; though he was just as eager to avoid her company, content to huddle with Gant, plotting his next attack on Hest, still stewing about Gudrum failing to kill his niece.

It was a surprise to see Osbert coming towards her, leading a fine-looking chestnut stallion whose mane had been braided, tail flicking impatiently, brown eyes full of fire. He reminded her of Tig, and Jael swallowed, wondering again what had happened to him.

'You didn't appear to be looking for a new horse,' Osbert said with a satisfied grin. 'So I found one for you.'

Jael frowned. '*Found* one?' The horse was a beauty, his warm brown coat glowing with a healthy sheen. She reached out a hand, placing it against his muzzle, and he pushed his head towards her, blowing softly. 'Just wandering around, was he? Lost?'

Osbert's grin grew. 'Well, I had Fitzig looking for just the right horse. I didn't imagine you'd be after a tame pony. Not a woman like you.' He held out the reins to Jael, puffing up his chest.

Jael took her hand away from the horse, eyeing her cousin

with disdain. 'You think you can buy my affection, Osbert? With a horse? When it was your father who gave away my horse in the first place? When you and Lothar took away everything my family had? You think I'll look favourably on because you found me a new horse? That I will *marry* you?' She snorted, angry, nostrils flaring. 'Will you just go and find another woman, Osbert!' she growled. 'There is nothing you could give me. Nothing that would ever make me marry a snivelling, spineless worm like you!'

A large crowd had gathered near the hall, and Jael spotted the look of alarm on her mother's face as she stood with Biddy, both of them clutching baskets to their chests, frozen to the spot.

But Jael couldn't take it back, and looking at the anger narrowing Osbert's scheming brown eyes, she didn't want to. He was a leech, hovering around whenever Aleksander disappeared, brushing against her, leering at her body, trying to ingratiate himself. She wanted him to stop. To get away from her.

To wake up and realise that she would never choose a husband like him.

She would never choose a husband at all.

Her eyes were up on the gates in the distance, and shivering, Jael tried to run, hobbling and limping, leaving Osbert and his horse behind, her mother and Biddy too. She hurried through the busy square, past Gant, who looked up, confusion in his eyes.

And then he was there.

Tig. Tig was there!

'Tig! Tig!' Tears in her eyes, Jael limped forward, not recognising the man who had brought him through the gates. Tig threw his head around, pleased to see her, though he sounded oddly quiet, and Jael could see the stitches on his back, and hurrying around him, looking him over, stitches zigzagging across his rump too.

'Found him wandering down the road,' the man said with a cheerful grin. 'Thought he might be lost. A fine horse like him? Looked like someone would be missing him.'

If Jael had had a silver coin, she would have given it to the man, though he winked at her, and she knew that Aleksander had likely already seen to that.

'What is going on?' Lothar's voice rose above the fray as more people clamoured to see what was happening. Most of them knew Tig. They knew Jael. It was Lothar and his children who were the strangers in Andala, though Lothar had brought enough men with him to ensure that what they thought was of little significance to him.

For now.

'Is that your *horse*?' Lothar's protruding eyes protruded even further. 'Where did he come from?' He spun around, poking his finger at the man's chest. The man, who was dressed like a farmer in a long brown cloak with a wide brim hat, was not from Andala, though he had known Ranuf Furyck, and he knew that his brother had usurped his throne.

He didn't step back.

'I found him on the road, my lord. Thought I'd bring him into the fort before I continued on to Vallsborg. Looked to me like he was someone's horse. Seems that I was right.' He smiled at Jael, who nodded her thanks and grabbed hold of Tig's bridle, forcing her eyes away from the gates, not wanting Lothar to think that she was waiting for Aleksander too. As far as he was concerned, Aleksander had already returned from hunting, and was back in the fort somewhere.

The looks on the faces of the Andalans gathered around them was one of surprise, happiness too. And Lothar did not want to cause problems for himself by stirring up trouble amongst those men and women he needed to support him.

Let her have her horse.

Let her have her cottage and her lover.

Let her have her brother, her mother, her grandmother, and that servant of hers too.

Because that was all Jael Furyck would ever have.

He would see to that.

And smiling, Lothar swept his fur-trimmed cloak around as he spun away.

***

Eirik stood on the hill overlooking the harbour. Conditions were fair for the first time in days, and two of his ships had returned that morning with whales.

Two whales.

Nearly everyone was down on the beach, working. Every part would be used. None would go to waste. Those whales would help sustain them over the winter.

But despite the relief he felt at the sight of those two enormous sea beasts, Eirik couldn't raise much more than half a smile. And he couldn't focus on what Morac was saying to him at all. 'Why not talk to Beorn?' he grumbled, at last, not wanting to be drawn out of his glum mood. He had been wracking his brain, trying to think of what to do with Eadmund. What to do about his throne.

He didn't want to think about ships. Not today.

Morac nodded. 'I will. I'm sure Otto will have some thoughts too.'

'I'm sure he will,' Eirik sighed, not turning to look at his friend as he headed back into the fort.

A cool breeze lifted the stink of the dead whales into the air, and Eirik was oddly reminded of his first wife and how she had hated the smell of whale blubber so much that she would vomit whenever she was near it.

It had not been his most successful marriage, he thought wryly, lost in the past again. And then a little cold hand, slipping into his. Eirik smiled, turning to look down on the shining black head of his precious daughter. 'You are like smoke, creeping around the fort. I never hear you coming!'

Eydis grinned. 'Maybe that's because your ears are filled with so much hair these days!'

'And how would you know?' Eirik wondered, slipping her cold hand through his arm, trying to warm it up. He turned her around, and they walked across the ridge, past the open gates of the old stone fort, not wanting to go inside.

'I see you in my dreams, Father,' Eydis said. 'Every night, I see you.'

That made Eirik both happy and sad. He knew what she saw sometimes, and he didn't want that for her. She was too young. Too innocent.

He squeezed her hand. 'Well, I shall have Frida give them a trim! I might start hearing like a young man again. Like Eadmund.' And then his smile was gone.

But Eydis' brightened.

'Last night I saw Eadmund,' she breathed, her body shivering with excitement. 'With a woman.'

'Oh?' Eirik lifted a wild white eyebrow. He didn't know what to say to that.

'I've seen her so many times. I didn't realise it, but she has been in my dreams for months. I saw her with Eadmund. Here. In the fort. With Eadmund. And he looked so different, Father. He was happy.'

Eirik didn't believe that such a thing sounded possible anymore. 'It wasn't Orla Berras, was it?' he joked. 'I don't want to relive that nightmare, thank you. I never want to hear that name again.'

'No.' Eydis shook her head, unable to stop smiling, despite her father's dour mood. 'It wasn't. It was Jael Furyck. I saw him with Jael Furyck!'

Eirik stumbled to a stop, and turning, he bent down to Eydis, eyes sharp now. 'What? But...' His mouth hung open, his head swivelling, looking from the old fort towards the bloody whales, hearing the thunderous roar of the harbour, seeing the murky waves assaulting the dark spires.

And Eirik's old blue eyes were suddenly moist.

He shook his head, laughing out loud. 'Jael Furyck! Ha! You're sure, Eydis? Sure it was her?'

'I am, Father. I saw it. She will come. Jael Furyck will come!'

THE END

EPILOGUE

'That door,' Jael grumbled, listening to the squeaking hinges as the cottage door rattled in a strong wind.

They had been lying in the dark for hours as the storm picked up, wondering if their little cottage would be able to withstand it.

Half hoping it wouldn't.

Aleksander smiled, holding Jael close, enjoying the feel of her, the smell of peppermint in her freshly washed hair. 'I'll fix it tomorrow. Promise.'

'You and your promises,' Jael yawned, entwining her legs around his. Her nose was frozen, her cheeks too, but under the fur with Aleksander, everything finally felt warm.

Right.

She almost didn't feel like wriggling away.

'I promised I'd bring Tig back, didn't I?'

Jael pushed herself up onto an elbow. She couldn't see anything more than shadows as she reached out a hand, running it over his hairy cheek. 'You did.' And leaning forward, she kissed him slowly, feeling the chill of his lips on hers, the coarse bristles of his beard brushing her skin. 'You did. And I'm so glad about that.' And lying back down again, Jael nestled in closer, not wanting to be anywhere else.

They could both hear Biddy snoring behind them; slightly singed Biddy who had finally managed to fall asleep after fussing around Aleksander for hours. He had stumbled into the cottage just as she was turning down the beds, starving, cold, and ready to fall asleep. Though both Biddy and Jael had managed to keep him awake long enough to hear about what had happened with Gudrum's men and the river.

Aleksander closed his eyes, exhausted. The arrow wound in his shoulder had leaked a lot of blood, and the ride home had been a slow and arduous one. He felt ready to sleep till Vesta. 'And now we can forget about Gudrum Killi.'

'For a while, at least,' Jael said, certain she would meet Gudrum again. Hopefully, when Lothar and his men weren't around to intervene. 'But I think we've got more pressing problems than that bastard, don't you?' She lowered her voice to just a breath. 'Like Lothar. And what he'll do next.'

'Something,' Aleksander decided, worry tensing his aching shoulder. 'He'll do something. He won't rest till he has you right where he wants you.'

'No, he won't. And where he wants me is ash, floating in the wind. If only he could figure out how to achieve it without damaging his reputation. Lucky for us, he's not as clever as he could be.'

The door banged against its frame, threatening to break apart, and Biddy woke up muttering. Neither Aleksander nor Jael spoke, and she quickly fell back to sleep.

'As long as we're together,' Aleksander whispered, leaning over Jael, wanting to feel her lips again. 'Lothar can never hurt us if we're together.'

Jael kissed him back, listening to the painful wail of the wind screeching around the cottage.

Suddenly unable to stop shivering.

BONUS CHAPTER

Discover what happens next in
The Furyck Saga Book One

WINTER'S
FURY

WINTER'S FURY: CHAPTER ONE

Jael Furyck's feet were freezing in wet socks that clung to numb toes, sitting in damp boots, which, although new, were already leaking. She tried to focus on her cold feet, pressing them harder into the wet wool; into the soft, damp leather of her boots; into the reeds that lined the hard mud floor. She imagined them twisting and strong, like the roots of Furia's Tree; buried deep in the earth, solid and unwavering. If she could just focus on her feet, then maybe she wouldn't say anything. Maybe there was a chance she could control the urgent, angry fire coursing up through her body and into her mouth.

No! Not her mouth, her feet, her feet!

She had to think of her feet.

She had to ignore the anger throbbing at the base of her throat, demanding to be released.

She couldn't let him, them, all of them, watch as she lost control.

Lothar Furyck perched impatiently on the edge of his ornately carved throne, glowering at his niece. His announcement moments earlier had all but guaranteed an explosive reaction from her, but where was it? Jael had a fierce temper, and this was to be the ultimate humiliation of her, and, by extension, her whole family, but so far, she would not play his carefully constructed game. Her face remained impassive, and although he was certain she was seething, she said nothing, which caused an uncomfortable silence to creep around them both. But Lothar had to say something or the moment would be lost to him. The Andalans sitting on their cold benches, looking up at their king would soon start to wonder what power he truly had over any of them. So biting down on his annoyance, Lothar cleared his throat and smiled as though there had been no awkward silence at all. 'And so, the wedding feast will take place on Oss in fifteen days. Plenty of time for you to find a dress!' He waved a chubby hand at Jael's well-worn trousers and cloak, nostrils flaring with distaste. 'And enough time for the rest of us to return to Andala before the Freeze sets in!'

Lothar leaned forward, his bulging eyes demanding a reply, and this time Jael knew that she had to say something. She couldn't just continue to ignore him. 'Will I be able to take my horse?' she asked dully, lips barely moving.

Lothar lifted an eyebrow, remembering how much trouble that horse had caused recently. It was better to be rid of them both. 'You may, but you will give up your sword. You won't be needing it where you're going.'

A surprised murmur echoed around the hall, sending another bolt of fury through Jael's rigid body. 'It was my father's sword,' she muttered haltingly, her devastation revealing itself at last.

'It was *my* father's sword,' Lothar growled, running a jewelled hand through his dark beard. 'The Furyck sword. Handed down from king to king. How or why you received it when my brother died, I do not know, you being neither his heir or a king.'

Jael wanted to launch herself at her uncle.

She wanted to rip out his vile throat, lying hidden beneath the rolls of fat gathering around his sagging chin. To watch his life-blood course down his bloated belly until he was white with death.

Take her sword?

She stood on the edge, ready to abandon all reason, but then, remembering her feet, Jael dug her toes deep into her boots, clenching her jaw. Lothar wasn't going to humiliate her any further. She wouldn't give him that. 'As you wish, Uncle.'

Lothar frowned, his shoulders sagging with disappointment. He'd watched his niece desperately trying to keep hold of her temper, and it appeared that she had succeeded. Though, he had hit his mark at least.

She was badly, if not fatally wounded.

Lothar could feel the growl of his dead brother at his back. Here he was, sitting on his brother's throne, selling his beloved daughter off to his enemy.

Just the thought of Ranuf's indignant face imbued Lothar with confidence, and the smile that curled his wet lips was wide and brimming with satisfaction. 'Good,' he said coolly, glancing at his son, Osbert, who was struggling to contain his own annoyance at Jael's oddly calm reaction. 'We will speak more of this tomorrow. Alp!' he barked, turning to his servant, who was hovering anxiously behind him, waiting to be called on. 'Have the next course brought out! And wine!' Lothar yelled as Alp turned and scurried towards the kitchen. 'I need more wine!'

Jael was rooted to the spot as the hall burst into life around her. The servants started moving again, ferrying trays of sizzling roast boar and pork sausages to the tables, filling cups with wine and ale as conversations sparked around them. It felt as though every pair of eyes was focused on her, and she was desperate to escape. Glancing around the hall, she spotted her mother, Gisila, lurking near one of the large fire pits, the shock of Lothar's announcement still on her pale face.

Jael made straight for her.

Gisila could feel the sting of tears in her eyes as she stared at the high table, watching Lothar and his vile son banging their cups together. It was sometimes hard to remember what it had felt like to sit up there with her husband, but she had, for thirty years, as his wife, the Queen of Brekka. Until Ranuf had died, and Lothar had returned to destroy all their lives.

Gisila felt a sudden pull from behind as Jael grabbed her by the arm and hurried her outside.

Dark clouds rushed across the moon. A storm was brewing, but Jael barely noticed as she stalked across the square, her hood pulled down to avoid the latecomers heading for the hall. Gisila walked quickly beside her, struggling to keep up with her daughter, conscious of the panic that was tightening her shoulders.

When they reached Gisila's small cottage, Jael ushered her mother inside, slamming the door behind them. Gisila's servant, Gunni, jumped in surprise, quickly making herself scarce, merging into the shadows at the back of the sparsely furnished hovel.

Dropping her hood, Jael turned to her mother, narrowing her intense green eyes until her eyebrows almost met in the middle of her face.

'I, I didn't know,' Gisila spluttered, sensing the angry fire that was coming. 'I didn't know!'

Jael was too wild to speak, her eyes sweeping the cottage with its hard mud floor, three low beds, a small fire for warmth and light, another for meals. There was a small kitchen area with a few shelves too, an old barrel for a table, five tree stumps for stools. It was windowless and dank, and utterly miserable, all of which likely delighted Lothar who appeared to take great pleasure in the demotion of his dead brother's family.

After stealing the throne from Ranuf's son, Lothar had kicked Gisila and her children out of the comfortable hall, moving his own family in. And now he presided over them like a tyrant, determined to squeeze every last bit of joy out of their lives.

Letting them live, but on his terms alone.

'What is Lothar thinking? You can't marry that man!' Gisila muttered crossly behind her. 'He is nothing. His family is nothing! His father was a slave. Ranuf's enemy and a slave! It's an insult. The worst Lothar has done to us for sure!'

That was just like her mother, Jael thought. Always making everything about herself.

'Where is Axl?' Gisila turned and directed this at Gunni who had started turning down the beds.

'I don't know, my lady.'

Gisila glanced at her daughter. 'Your brother will have something to say about this, I'm sure.'

Jael said nothing. Her head was a mess of hot fury and building sorrow. She couldn't keep up with her thoughts as they tumbled over one another, desperately seeking a way out of the hole that Lothar had so happily trapped her in. Running her hands through her long dark hair, mostly tied up in messy braids, Jael frowned. Surely she was too old for marriage? And why would Eirik Skalleson of all people want her for his son?

Why now?

Jael turned to the door. 'I'll go and see Edela. She'll know what to do.' And ducking her head, she slipped outside before her mother had even looked up.

The wind whipped the door shut with such a bang that Gisila jumped, and folding her arms across her chest to ward off the chill, she returned her gaze to the fire. There was nothing her mother could say that would stop this, she was certain. Lothar had finally found a way to remove Jael, and with her gone, they would all be exposed, for Jael was their protector, and Lothar knew it. Without her, they were weak and vulnerable.

Just as he intended.

Gisila shivered, eyes lost in the twisting flames, tears running down her cold cheeks.

***

Jael strode up the path to her grandmother's old cottage which sat up a small rise, slippery with patches of ice. A line of bones and stones strung about the porch chimed chaotically to announce her arrival.

Axl opened the door, smiling in surprise to see his sister, although the look on her face quickly soured his. 'Jael? Are you alright?' he frowned. She didn't reply, staring past his gangly frame into the dull glow of Edela's cottage. Axl knew well enough not to prod any further. 'I was just leaving,' he mumbled, squeezing past his tall sister and out into the night. Wrapping his cloak around a pair of broad shoulders, he walked carefully down the path, wondering if his mother knew what was wrong with Jael.

Edela Saeveld sat in her fur-thick chair, just to the right of a low-burning fire. She studied her granddaughter with one raised eyebrow, patting the stool in front of her. 'Well, come on, then, you may as well tell me what your storm is about tonight,' she smiled, her weathered face creasing with an easy humour, which, she noticed, did little to change the fierceness of the face considering her.

Jael didn't sit down.

Edela frowned, her smile disappearing. 'What has happened, Jael? Tell me.'

'Well, you're the dreamer, Grandmother,' Jael grumbled. 'Why don't you tell me? Why *didn't* you tell me? You see everything that's going to happen. Why didn't you see this?' She clenched her jaw, trying to calm herself down, knowing that Lothar was the one she was truly angry at.

Edela blinked, small blue eyes full of confusion before they suddenly cleared. 'Ahhh, so Lothar is marrying you off, then?'

'You knew?' Jael's eyes bulged. 'Of course you knew!'

Edela stood, grimacing at the familiar ache in her right hip as she hobbled towards her granddaughter. 'I will make you some tea, and you will sit down, and we will talk. If you wish to yell, Jael, go and yell at the moon. It is full enough out there to hear you, I'm sure, even over that screeching wind.' And with that, she bustled away to her kitchen corner, rummaging around the overfilled shelves, heaving with pots and cups, fresh and dried herbs, and all sorts of strange items that no one dared ask about. Edela was more than a dreamer, gifted with visions of the future, she was Andala's healer, called upon to cure all manner of ailments. And, after twenty-seven years of looking after Jael, she had grown quite used to easing red-hot tempers.

Jael sighed. Experience told her that there was no shifting her grandmother, so moving the stool closer to the fire, she sat down, her body humming with an urgency to run out into the night and stab her sword through one of Lothar's bulbous eyes.

If he wanted the Furyck sword so much, he could have it.

Marry her to an Islander? Send her away from Brekka?

And what about Aleksander?

Edela came back with a cup and handed it to Jael before lifting her cauldron from its hook, carefully pouring hot water over the fragrant herbs she had sprinkled inside. 'Here, let this sit a while, then have a good drink. It will help with all that fire in there.' She waved at Jael's creased forehead as she replaced the small cauldron, and slunk back into her chair.

'Thank you,' Jael mumbled. 'Now, tell me everything.'

Edela laughed, leaning back, feeling the comforting warmth of fur beneath her bones. 'Everything?' She smiled, rubbing her cold hands together. 'Well, I knew you would be married one day. Yes, I did see that.'

'And you didn't think to *tell* me?' Jael was incredulous, almost spilling the hot tea. 'Grandmother! Why didn't you tell me? I could have done something! Aleksander and I could have made plans to leave! Years ago! We could have done something! Anything but this!'

Edela inhaled the sweet scents of skullcap and chamomile as they steeped in Jael's cup. 'Yes, I could have told you,' she said calmly. 'But being a dreamer is not about revealing everything you see. It's not as simple as that,' she sighed. 'And yes, of course, you could have run away. But in my dreams, I saw you with this man. I saw that it was meant to be. There is something about you and him together that is important somehow. I know it's not what you wanted, but it was clear to me that this marriage was fated. I had no choice but to stay quiet.'

'*What?*' Jael shook her head. 'No. No! You should have told me! You should have given *me* a choice. You should have left it up to *me* to decide!'

Edela sat, untroubled by Jael's bellowing. 'Perhaps. Perhaps you would have found your way to him anyway? But who am I to take that risk? To interfere with the plans the gods have made for you? And not your gods either, Jael, but mine. The Tuuran gods show me my dreams, and I am bound to do their bidding. They believe that you belong with this man, so who am I to argue?'

Jael scowled. Her grandmother had guided and advised her throughout her life. Her visions had always come true – well, those that she had told her about, at least – so there was no reason to doubt her now. 'But Eadmund Skalleson? Eadmund the Drunkard?' she snorted. '*That's* the husband your gods see me with? Are you sure you have the right man?'

'Well...' Edela admitted with a twinkle in her eye, 'that part of my dream is a little hazy, but yes, Eadmund Skalleson. He is the one I have always seen.'

'The one?' Jael wanted to vomit. She absentmindedly sipped the hot tea, grimacing as it scalded the tip of her tongue.

'Well, he hasn't always been known by that name, has he? He was Eadmund the Bold when you fought him all those years ago.'

Jael tried to recall the fleeting moment she had trapped him beneath her sword, but it was too long ago, and she didn't remember him at all. She gritted her teeth, overcome by another burst of rage. 'No! I'm not going to do it! I'm not going to leave Andala! What about Axl? Who will look after him? Or you, or Mother? And what about Aleksander...' Her angry eyes softened suddenly, and she sighed.

Edela reached out and took Jael's hand, her eyes full of sympathy.

Jael snatched it back. 'You never thought Aleksander and I were meant to be together. I know that,' she said harshly.

'No,' Edela admitted. 'That is true, as much as I love you both. But you and Eadmund, I believe, *are* meant to be. I have dreamed about this since you were born.' She stared earnestly at her granddaughter. 'I know it for certain, Jael. He is the father of the child you will have.'

Edela's words were delivered so quietly that Jael almost didn't hear her, but shock quickly flooded her face. '*Child*?' she breathed, as realisation dawned. 'And you see *that* as my future? A mother? A wife?'

'Yes, there is that, but you will have your sword also, of that I have no doubt.'

'Well, not according to Lothar.'

Edela raised her eyebrows. 'Things are not always as they seem. Our lives shift and change like the clouds. Nothing stands still,' she smiled. 'I see you with a sword. Do not worry.'

Jael felt confused, if not slightly heartened by that news.

But a child? With Eadmund the Drunkard?

How was she going to tell Aleksander?

***

Osbert was drunk.

Drunk and pissing against the side of the blacksmith's shed, when he saw Jael heading in his direction. Blinking to try and clear his blurry vision, he shook off his dripping cock, resettling his fur cloak. Sucking in his bloated belly, he stepped out into the street, snatching his cousin's arm as she flew by.

Jael jerked around in surprise, wrenching her arm out of his grip. Seeing that it was Osbert, she was eager to be gone, but he reached out and grabbed her again, his sharp fingernails pinching her skin. She glared down at him, her face betraying no sign of the discomfort he was causing. 'What do you want, Osbert?' she fumed as the wind screamed between them.

He almost stumbled then, his footing uncertain in the thick mud, but righting himself quickly, he narrowed his eyes. 'This could all have been so different, Jael,' he slurred through freezing lips. 'You need not have become a pawn in my father's game. You could have stayed here in Andala, as you always wanted to. As Queen of Brekka. As my wife.' He was leaning closer now, his sour spittle blowing over her.

Jael curled away from him, yanking her arm free. 'You think *you'd* make a better husband than Eadmund the Drunkard? That I'd rather have Osbert the Coward in my bed?' she snorted. 'No, Cousin, your father has made me a much better match than you would ever have been.'

Her words slapped Osbert across the face, and colour rose in his cheeks as he tried to contain his anger. 'If you say so, Jael,' he sneered, eyeing her threateningly. 'But just remember that while you're on Oss with your new husband, your fat belly, and your runt litter of slave princes, I'll be here watching over *your* family.' His satisfaction bloomed as he watched fear spark in Jael's eyes. 'You never know what accident may befall them if you're not careful. I'd hate for you to lose another member of your dwindling family.' His threat delivered, Osbert stumbled away from his cousin, heading for the hall, where he planned to warm his bones and drown the miserable bitch out of his head once and for all.

***

Aleksander was waiting when Jael arrived back at Gisila's cottage, his dark eyes troubled. He wasn't easy to anger and even now, when faced with losing her, he managed to retain an unnatural level of calm. They had been inseparable for seventeen years, lovers for the past twelve. He wouldn't accept that this was the end.

He couldn't lose her.

'Jael.' Aleksander came towards her as she entered the cottage, but Jael's arms remained firmly by her sides as she stopped before him.

She could barely look at Aleksander's face. His thick eyebrows twitched above a pair of hooded deep-brown eyes, almost black, and so full of concern. Dropping her head, she hurried to warm her hands by the fire, where she waited, trying to think of what to say to any of them. Eventually, shivering as some feeling returned to her body, Jael turned around.

'What did Edela have to say?' Gisila wondered anxiously. She'd been talking about nothing else since Axl and Aleksander had arrived.

Jael ignored her. 'Where were you?' she asked, staring accusingly at Aleksander.

He was surprised by that.

'Hunting. I told you before I left,' he answered defensively, coming to join Jael by the fire. 'I went to the hall to find you. Gant told me what had happened, so I came straight here.'

'You're back late.'

'The weather's closing in. I could barely see. I wasn't going to risk Ren by pushing him too hard.' He shook his head, feeling confused. Worried. 'I'm sorry I wasn't there when Lothar made his... announcement.'

Jael swallowed at the reminder, dismissing his words. She felt angry at Aleksander. Unfairly so. What could he have done to make anything different?

What could any of them have done?

'Jael.' Gisila was insistent now. 'What did your grandmother say?'

Jael sighed, walking a treacherous path in her mind. 'She... she thought it was... the right thing to happen. She'd seen it in her dreams, that it was the... right thing.' Jael couldn't say any more. She looked into a dark corner of the cottage, her head swirling with confusion.

Aleksander's face fell.

Jael had always been an impossibly stubborn woman; always working on a plan. If she believed in a cause, she would fight and never give in. He'd witnessed that enough times. But now, as she hung her head and hid her face from him, he knew.

And turning for the door, Aleksander headed out of the cottage.

Jael spun around to see the door hanging open in his wake.

Her shoulders drooped.

This was not going to be easy, whichever path she decided to take.

'The right thing?' Axl looked confused as he strode over to face his sister, who was almost as tall as he was. Almost as tall as their father had been. 'How is this the right thing for any of us? You'll be lost to Brekka forever! There'll be no hope of me taking the throne from Lothar without you, which, of course, he knows.' He felt angry and frustrated. He'd imagined that Jael would do anything to stay in Andala. That she would never give up the chance to reclaim their father's throne.

To defeat Lothar and Osbert, and get them out of Brekka for good.

He didn't understand her lack of reaction at all.

Jael rounded on her brother. 'How will my staying here change anything?' Heated now by the warmth of the cottage and her own discomfort, she removed her cloak and threw it over a stool, leaving the fire to stand further away, uncertain how or where to be. 'What have *we* been able to do to weaken Lothar's position since he arrived?' she whispered hoarsely. Lothar's spies were everywhere, and she didn't want the wind carrying her words out into the night. 'He has the army behind him. He turned all of Father's men against us. There's nothing here for us. No future. No hope. It's gone, Axl!' She gestured around the tiny cottage. 'Does this look like the home of Brekka's royal family anymore?'

'Well, we won't know now, will we?' Axl spat, his temper rising to match hers.

Jael stepped towards her brother, glaring into his simmering hazel eyes. 'You think there's something I could do to change this?' she demanded. 'Kill Lothar? And then, what? Kill Osbert? And how would his men respond to that? Happily? I don't think so. Or, we could run, but where would we go? Lothar has allies in nearly every kingdom, and those he isn't allied with would still turn us in. No one wants Brekka for an enemy. We would never be safe! Is that what you want? For our family to run until we're hunted down and slaughtered? Can you see Edela living like that? Mother? Biddy?'

'Stop!' Gisila implored, coming between her two children. 'Come and sit down, both of you. This is no night to be on different sides. We must stay united if we're to stay alive.' She sighed deeply. The sudden change in their circumstances had left her feeling so much older than her fifty-two years. Her long dark hair was thick with silver strands. Her once much-admired figure was frail and thin. She had been the Queen of Brekka for thirty years. Married to Ranuf, a man she had fought and argued with, loved and despised in equal measure. The shame of being reduced to this lesser existence had damaged her pride, and the loss of her husband had broken her spirit. But she had hope still, and that hope was living within Jael and Axl. And she knew that the way back to her rightful place in Brekka was through them.

If only she could keep them believing that.

'And what about you, Mother?' Jael wondered sharply. 'Why didn't you know that any of this was coming?'

Gisila looked surprised. 'Why would I?'

'You and Lothar are very friendly,' Axl said, joining his sister. 'Especially since Rinda died.'

'Not like that, we're not! Nor have we ever been! Lothar may wish for things, but I am no slave, and he won't get anything from me that I do not wish to give. And I do not wish to give *that*!'

'Still, you've always been close to him, Mother.' Jael wasn't letting go that easily.

'And if I am?' Gisila whispered crossly. 'I need to keep us all safe. It's not just the two of you who are thinking of our future.' She shook her head, tears leaking into the heavy creases around her swollen eyes. 'I'm trying to keep us all alive! Do you think I want to do that? Placate the man who stole the throne from you, Axl? No, I do what I must to protect us all. It isn't easy, but what choice do I have? What choice do any of us have?'

Tears slid down Gisila's face, and Axl, who hated seeing his mother cry, put an arm around her shoulder.

Jael stared blankly at the door, wondering where Aleksander had gone; wanting to be with him but at the same time desperate to grab her horse and ride until she couldn't be found. Inside her head, she could hear herself screaming to find a way out, but Edela's words echoed too, imploring her to keep to the path before her. The path that only Edela and her gods could see.

Beside her, Gisila sobbed, and Axl simmered.

And Aleksander had gone.

WINTER'S FURY

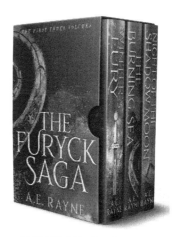

WINTER'S FURY
The Furyck Saga: Book One

THE FURYCK SAGA
Books: One - Three

SERIES ORDER

WINTER'S FURY
The Furyck Saga: Book One

THE BURNING SEA
The Furyck Saga: Book Two

NIGHT OF THE SHADOW MOON
The Furyck Saga: Book Three

HALLOW WOOD
The Furyck Saga: Book Four

THE RAVEN'S WARNING
The Furyck Saga: Book Five

VALE OF THE GODS
The Furyck Saga: Book Six

Sign up to my newsletter, so you don't miss out
on new release information!

http://www.aerayne.com/sign-up

ABOUT A.E. RAYNE

Upon discovering that her chances for inventing a time machine were rather slim, eight-year-old A.E. Rayne decided to pursue a career as a writer instead. She completed a Bachelor of Communication Studies, majoring in television, then trained as a graphic designer, while dabbling in poetry, and continually plotting her first novel.

A.E. Rayne survives on a happy diet of historical and fantasy fiction and particularly loves a good Viking tale.
Her favourite authors are Bernard Cornwell, Giles Kristian, Robert Low, C.J. Sansom, and Patrick O'Brian.

She lives in Auckland, New Zealand with her husband, three children and two dogs.

Kings of Fate is a prequel novella in her epic fantasy series, *The Furyck Saga*.

To find out more about A.E. Rayne and her writing visit her website: www.aerayne.com

Printed in Great Britain
by Amazon

69241329R00109